Talon

A chronicle of history and love, of dreams and healing power. A mystery of human tragedy and loss. The reader stumbles through fire, a circle that opens and finally closes again. A work so spare yet so full, delightful in its poetry and lyricism. A great novel.

—John Weier

Paulette has honoured the travel to the underbelly of her dreams. She's done so with fierce courage and was rewarded with these voices which now speak . . . let her story weave its magic and its mystery to your visions.

—SkyDancer Louise Bernice Halfe

Talon

PAULETTE DUBÉ

NeWest Press

National Library of Canada Cataloguing in Publication Data
Dubé, Paulette, 1963-
Talon

(Nunatak fiction)
ISBN 1-896300-47-2

I. Title. II. Series.
PS8557.U2323T34 2002   C813'.54   C2002-910990-6
PR9199.3.D81T34 2002

Editor for the Press: Thomas Wharton
Text editor: Carol Berger
Cover and interior design: Ruth Linka
Cover image: Yvonne Blanchette
Author photo: Raymond Blanchette-Dubé

Some of the poems contained herein have appeared in slightly different form in, *the house weighs heavy,* from Thistledown Press. The poems, "Mr. Nobody," Phélice's "Prayer Before Sleep," and "Now The Day Is Over," are from the book: *Poems for Boys and Girls Book One,* Edited by Grace Morgan and C.B. Routley, The Copp Clark Publishing Co. Limited, Toronto, 1955.

I have taken liberties with some of the information contained in the following texts: Histoire de Legal History Association, *Vision Courage Heritage,* First Printing, Legal, Alberta, 1995; *Official Farmer's Almanac,* 1987.

Canadian   Patrimoine
Heritage   canadien

NeWest Press acknowledges the support of the Canada Council for the Arts and the Alberta Foundation for the Arts for our publishing program. We also acknowledge the financial support of the Government of Canada through the Book Publishing Industry Development Program (BPIDP) for our publishing activities.

NeWest Press
201–8540–109 Street
Edmonton, Alberta
T6G 1E6
(780) 432-9427
www.newestpress.com

1 2 3 4 5 06 05 04 03 02

PRINTED AND BOUND IN CANADA

In the end, what we need to survive is maimed, burnt, and broken but refuses to be forgotten.

Pour faire une tresse—assemblez trois longues mèches de cheveux;

une pour l'âme

une pour la raison

et une pour l'action.

She's sitting in her chair.
The rocking chair in the kitchen.

She slowly licks the palm of her left hand
then licks between the fingers
curving her tongue over the skin web
like Marc used to do when he loved her.

She thinks of her brothers
she thinks of her son Raoul—gone away, safe to grow up in Montana
safe from the vicious traps
her neighbour's are setting.

The clock is ticking.
It chimes 7:30.

It's not her fault Zoë Trefflé wasn't able to keep the baby.
Not her fault the baby died.
Not her fault Zoë died.
She had done what she could,
warning Zoë against the drink,
warning her that Télèsphore bothering her all the time would hurt the baby,
weaken her.
And working around those sick cows was asking for trouble,
but Zoë wouldn't listen.

And now she knew tonight,
tonight they would come
under cover of the new moon
led by the drunken courage and useless fury of Télèsphore Trefflé.
They would come and they would kill her.

She hears footsteps on the frozen ground.

She hears Antoine Trefflé calling her names. She hears Télèsphore cursing,
stomping his boots on the small porch, then crashing into the door. He

comes in a rush towards her, ready with the ropes, but stops clumsily when she rises from her chair and turns her back to him. The others crowd in behind him, pushing him forward. They smell of ragotte, burped-over pork and cabbage. She cannot bear to see them look at her as if she is an animal they must hunt and kill. Their fear has a smell that threatens to choke her, make her cry.

She turns when she hears Télèsphore's laboured breathing and knows the lung infection has not cleared. With no one to help him, he will be dead before the year is out.

Antoine catches sight of the ghost smile creeping. He slaps her across the face, screaming about her arrogance, and the others laugh loudly, slapping each other on the back.

Télèsphore grabs the jug of ragotte from Antoine and spins Rubis around to face the men. She stumbles forward. A young boy near the door makes a little movement towards her, but Télèsphore curses him to keep his place.

—I told you to keep yourself quiet! he bellows. —The Almighty Madame Rubis Morin, the cursed healer, does not need your help, little Baptiste. Here, Healer, you want something? You want some help? Take some of this, he slurs, wrenching her chin back with his free hand and shoving the jug into her face. —This, this is my medicine. This is holy water. Let's see what good it does you.

Rubis jerks her head away and crosses her arms, saying nothing.

—I said drink, goddamn you, he snarls, gripping her arm and splashing the alcohol.

Rubis splutters and coughs, the liquid burning her eyes and mouth.

Antoine steps forward. —Don't waste it, for Chrissake. If she don't want it Télèsphore, I do!

He wrestles the jug from his brother's grip and tips it eagerly to his own mouth.

—Come on, Télèsphore barks, —I didn't come here for no party. We got things to do, einh? he leers. —We came here to do something, so let's do it.

He yanks the rope expertly around her wrists, hobbling her to her own ankles.

—Come on bitch, you're coming with us, he snarls, pushing her toward the door.

The men shove themselves up against her as she passes, rubbing their hands on her body and laughing about a waste of good meat. Télèsphore ignores them, pulls her roughly behind him into the night.

They take her through the yard and up the road, more roughly than is necessary. They need to hear her cry or plead, whimper or shout, anything to show that they have finally broken her. Rubis says nothing. She keeps her eyes on the ground, refusing to give them the satisfaction of knowing she is already broken.

They drink heavily from the flasks they'd filled at Trefflé's earlier. They shout obscenities to egg each other on and pull her along, jerking on the rope to make her stumble.

They gather stones along the way, large blue field stones.

They bring her to water.

Six-year-old Baptiste Trefflé stays in the deepest shadows.

a woman
slow eyes of the most kissing blue
long red hair flowing down to the middle of her back
field stones in a bag around her waist
heavy, chafing rope binds her wrists

thrown in from above
somehow
shoes and all

lungs filling with water

fire in her veins
bubbles—
huge silver balloons
filled with fire

within twelve heartbeats

                              "J'entends le moulin"

within twelve breaths

                              "tique, tique, taque."

an open mouth

                              "J'entends le moulin"

a circle mute

                              "taque"

her dress up above her face

                              "Mon père a fait bâtir maison"

her hands open in front of her

                              "l'a fait bâtir à trois pignons"

then

                              "tique, tique, tique, taque"

the woman
folds over herself
and the power
they cursed as evil

blinks once

like a star

and is gone

                              "tique, tique, taque."

J'entends le moulin, tique, tique taque.
J'entends le moulin, taque.

So sings Rubis softly as she begins to braid her hair.

Talon, Alberta 1962

The phone rings, Léonie jumps. Breathlessly, she moves to stop its intrusive shrilling. She speaks to Madelaine. Yes, yes, they are on their way right now.

–Phélice! Hurry up, for goodness sake, they're waiting for us! she calls nervously, hanging up the phone.

She quickly stuffs the book back into her daughter's bag and shakily pours out two cups of coffee. She catches sight of a spider disappearing into the handbag.

–Mom? Can I borrow this sweater? Or maybe this jacket, what do you think?

Léonie hurries down the hallway, sloshing coffee from the too-full cups.

–Here, she says, offering Phélice a cup, pushing open the bedroom door with her hip, –maybe this will light a fire under you . . .

Inside the church the families take their places on the benches bought by their grandparents years ago.

Phélice sits beside her mother. Further along, taking up the rest of the Morin bench, are the two sets of twins Patrique told her about in the car. Phélice keeps leaning forward to catch glimpses of her aunts, until her mother settles her down, like a wayward child, by quietly reaching for her hand and stroking it gently.

Feeling chastised but unable to contain herself, Phélice leans over to her mother and whispers, –They sure look alike, don't they?

Léonie frowns at her.

–Don't they? repeats Phélice, again leaning forward.

–Phélice! her mother says sharply, –Have a little respect!

She drops Phélice's hand and stares fixedly at the coffin at the front of the church.

Contrite, Phélice picks up her mother's hand and settles back on the bench. She stares at the coffin, conjuring her grandmother's face and noble bearing.

"Overbearing is more like it," hears Phélice.

Aurore leans forward. She catches Phélice's eye and winks, then fades back beside Madelaine.

Phélice's mouth hangs open. What just happened here? she thinks wildly. Did she hear me? Did I say that out loud? . . . no, it can't be. Aurore is just an old woman, bent over her rosary, counting the red cut-glass beads, mouthing the words "Je crois en Dieu, le Père tout puissant, Créateur du ciel et de la terre . . ."

The words are spoken in time with the rhythmic clicking of rosary beads from all over the church. Phélice thinks of pebbles chunkling on the bottom of a creek bed. She and Philia are picking mint. She hears her mémère's voice.

Talon 1961

—Watch out there, the nettles on that one really sting.

—Yes, Mémère.

—Bring me that other basket, would you?

Phélice bends over, wincing. She hides her grimace by exaggerating her limp and crossing her eyes.

—Yes, Grand Mathter, here you are, she lisps playfully.

Philia looks up, smiles. Then her eyes narrow and she grabs Phélice by the wrist, pulling the girl's sleeve up to her elbow. Her sharp intake of breath is the only outward sign of the revulsion she feels when she sees her grand-daughter's bruised arm.

—What happened? she asks softly, running a gnarled finger over the tender skin.

—I bruise easy, you know that, Phélice tries to shrug her sleeve back down. —I must have slept funny and . . .

—Pretty funny, all right. You sleep on stones? You sleep while people pelt you with stones?

Phélice laughs uneasily, —Well, no, not exactly, not stones, not really.

—Pierre, Philia says flatly, looking away from Phélice, her jaw tightening.

—We were just fooling around . . . he doesn't realize that it hurts me, he just grabs a little too hard sometimes.

She pulls her wrist gently from Philia's grasp and gingerly smoothes her sleeves down.

Nothing escapes Philia's scrutiny. —Those bruises aren't all that's wrong. Where else did he hurt you, ma fille?

Phélice busies herself with the mint in front of her. Her eyes begin to blur as she shakes her head no. The slaps to her stomach tighten, the kicks to the back of her legs strain. Phélice just shakes her head no.

—Phélice? Phélice look at me. Philia's tone is warm.

Phélice wants to throw herself into her grandmother's arms and stay there, protected forever, but she stands rooted to the spot.

—Phélice, you don't deserve this. No more than your mother deserved what she ate from your father's plate, mutters Philia.

Phélice's head shoots up. My father? My father did this to Maman? She opens her mouth to speak, but Philia holds up her hand to quiet her.

—Some men are animals, worse than pigs; it is not right to hit a woman. Pierre should not hurt you. I won't let him Phélice. Do you understand? Philia's voice is low and carries a warning note. —He cannot be allowed to hurt you again.

Phélice nods her head, wiping her tears away with the back of her hand.

—We won't talk about this. You don't have to afraid anymore. He has hit you for the last time, I promise you that.

—Mémère, I, Maman, what about . . . she looks at Philia, who meets her eyes.

—Not now, chouette, not now. Now, she says picking up the basket at her feet, —we have to get back and get lunch going. The others will wonder where we've gone off to. Can't have them calling the police on us, now can we? Philia's voice is smiling, her eyes are not.

—But when? asks Phélice, aware that she is asking two things at once.

—Soon, ma fille, soothes Philia, threading her arm gently through Phélice's, —soon.

Phélice flips to the front of her mother's small, well-worn Bible. Léonie hauls it out for baptisms, weddings, and funerals, says she would rather read than listen to the priest. Phélice runs her finger along the names listed there, a family tree:

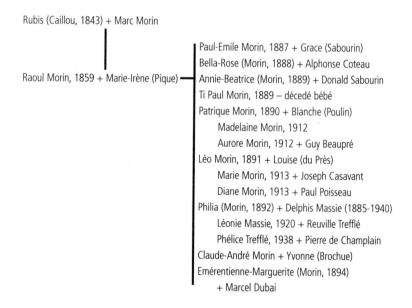

Rubis (Caillou, 1843) + Marc Morin

Raoul Morin, 1859 + Marie-Irène (Pique) —

Paul-Emile Morin, 1887 + Grace (Sabourin)
Bella-Rose (Morin, 1888) + Alphonse Coteau
Annie-Beatrice (Morin, 1889) + Donald Sabourin
Ti Paul Morin, 1889 – décedé bébé
Patrique Morin, 1890 + Blanche (Poulin)
    Madelaine Morin, 1912
    Aurore Morin, 1912 + Guy Beaupré
Léo Morin, 1891 + Louise (du Près)
    Marie Morin, 1913 + Joseph Casavant
    Diane Morin, 1913 + Paul Poisseau
Philia (Morin, 1892) + Delphis Massie (1885-1940)
    Léonie Massie, 1920 + Reuville Trefflé
    Phélice Trefflé, 1938 + Pierre de Champlain
Claude-André Morin + Yvonne (Brochue)
Emérentienne-Marguerite (Morin, 1894)
    + Marcel Dubai

Hmmm, thinks Phélice, we are going to have to erase that name soon, aren't we? Monsieur Pierre de Champlain, no thank you. She licks her thumb and tries to smudge the ink. Léonie looks over and although she smiles at her daughter, she gently takes the book from her.

They begin the mass. Everyone follows the steps they could repeat in their sleep, the ritualistic standing, sitting, kneeling. They answer when they are spoken to, they sing, they cross themselves, and keep their heads bowed.

When they come to the new part in the ceremony, where everyone is supposed to shake hands, most of the old people simply smile to the person beside them and refuse to acknowledge those they hate. They are not hypocrites. These people know that God sees everything, all the time, and shaking hands with people you despise in your heart is a lie.

They turn easily enough towards each other though; Madelaine kisses Aurore, Aurore kisses Marie who kisses Diane, and on down through the line, until Léonie turns to her own daughter and kisses her. Phélice leans towards her mother and sneaks a look down the row at her aunts. Well, they aren't really my aunts are they? she thinks. They are my uncles' daughters, Patrique and Léo are Mom's uncles . . . so really, they are what to me?

Taking advantage of the rustle that follows the ritualistic acknowledgement of kinsmen, Phélice whispers to Léonie. ‒Mom? I loved Mémère, you know. She was very good to me. She always seemed to know exactly what to do . . . she trails off, uncertain of how her mother will react, willing her mother to continue the conversation.

‒Yes, Philia Massie was never without an opinion or a way to make her opinion known. She took care of us, all of us as best she could. La famille, notre famille, la sainte famille, says Léonie chuckling softly, one eye on her daughter and one on the priest at the front.

The priest squints in their direction, they both lower their heads.

Phélice smiles and begins plucking at the thread that hangs from a button on her sweater. It unravels quickly, too quickly, and Phélice is left grasping the end of the thread while the button goes skipping down the row.

Clémence leans forward and scoops up the button. She turns it around in her hands and, smiling, shows it to Aurore.

▦ Talon, Alberta 1932

Aurore remembers when Clémence first came to live with them.

—Do you have a big garden, Madame? asks Clémence once we've rounded the house. We are off to pick wild strawberries for supper.

—Oh, it's a fair size I suppose. But this garden belongs to both of us, Madelaine and I. We share the patch between our two houses. We thought it would cut down on the work that way. See that house over there? That's my house. I live there with my husband, M Guy Beaupré. We farm this section and Madelaine farms the west half, just over that way, past that little stand of birch.

—Where are your children, Madame Aurore? Clémence asks shyly.

I stop and look at her, walking away from me slowly, as if I am still beside her. She walks four steps away from me and when she turns back, I answer, —I carry my children like you will carry yours, Clémence. I carry them here, I trace my fingertip over the wrinkles on my cheeks, —and here, I finger a scar above my right eye, —and here, I touch a deep furrow between my eyes. —They are never very far away, really. Come, I'll show you.

We walk towards the birch. The ground is scattered with lily of the valley. Crocuses bloom between small, white wooden crosses.

Clémence gazes at the thirty or so crosses clustered together near the centre, fanning outward. —Are these all your babies, Madame? she whispers uneasily.

I shake my head, laughing. —Heavens no! How old do you think I am? I may be unlucky around the edges, but this, I swing my arms wide, —this is the bad luck of the whole village. These little ones weren't ready to stay born. So we . . . Ah! There's Madelaine.

Madelaine has been tending one of the gravesites. She quickly straightens when she hears our voices.

—Aurore! snaps Madelaine. —What are you doing here? You, she glares at Clémence, —you shouldn't be here. And why are you wearing my sweater?

—Madame Aurore said I should, I mean, I am sorry I didn't ask, . . . I . . . stutters Clémence.

—Voyons, Madelaine! I cough politely, waving lazily at a fly. —The girl needed a little sweater and yours, though in bad need of buttons, was there beside the door as we left. We came to pick strawberries for supper. We were just talking, you know, just looking . . .

—Listen girl, Madelaine points to Clémence, —there are no strawberries here. What grows here are crosses. When you speak of this place, and you will, I need you, she pauses, —we need you, to have it right. The truth. Are you ready for the truth?

Clémence opens her mouth but nothing comes out. She looks in terror and confusion from Madelaine to me.

I see she has the sudden urge to pee.

—Back there, I nod.

Clémence smiles gratefully before scurrying off behind a bush, the sweater snagging on the rough, still unfinished cross that serves to mark the place of my poor little Johanna.

—Madelaine, I . . .

—Aurore, I blame you for this. Why did you bring her here? I don't need her spreading lies. Enough of that around here already, snaps Madelaine.

—Don't you trust her, Madelaine?

I hope this doesn't sound like teasing to Madelaine, I know how serious this is.

—Oh, it's not that, she's a good girl, says Madelaine, suddenly flustered. —It's just that, well . . . she flutters her hands, —she's still a stranger, Aurore. A stranger who is a Trefflé, she finishes softly, her hands falling to her sides.

—Madelaine, I try to reassure her by resting my hand on her arm, —we have dealt with them before, and I know young Clémence will be around for a long time. She will be like family to me and you and the others . . . to

Léonie. I think this . . . I sweep my arm to embrace the small graveyard, —Clémence has to know about this. You know that. She has memories here too now, after all that bleeding.

Madelaine shakes her head and takes my hand. —I don't like it, she mutters, she is not . . .

—Going to do any damage to that old sweater of yours? I think if you ask her, she may even sew some buttons on that ratty old thing for you. Will you, Clémence? I ask, as Clémence emerges from the bushes, pulling cobwebs from her hair.

—Oui, Madame Aurore, of course. If you'd like me too, I will, she says eagerly, trying to clean the sweater of dry leaves and spider webs.

—No buttons, just leave it, grunts Madelaine. —I like it the way it is.

I trample the grass to make a sort of nest so we can sit comfortably, and not surprise any spiders. We have loads of time before supper is ready. Clémence sits down beside me. Pulling her skirts over her knees and resting her head on her knees, she half closes her eyes.

Madelaine looks around her, checking the position of the sun. She sighs, taken in by the calmness and beauty of this place, she too sits down.

—Non, strawberries do not grow here, there isn't enough sun, she grunts amiably. —This place has very rich soil though, very good for flowers.

She tilts her head with magpie-like scrutiny towards Clémence. —You know we put bodies down here, einh? You know that because you can see the crosses, and Aurore already told you that much I suppose. But you can you see the most important thing? Can you see the reason they are here? Can you see the babies? she asks. —We planted lily of the valley here. Crocuses bloom here by themselves. We can see them, we smell them. The babies are in the flowers, sometimes because of the flowers. We carry them with us in our skin, she whispers, leaning forward, lightly touching the small wrinkle at the corner of Clémence's mouth.

Clémence's hand goes to her mouth, her eyes wide.

I pick at a thread on my sweater and continue, —The priest refused to bless this ground, said it was "outside the Church." Said the babies died in perpetual sin. Children in limbo are never baptized. We snuck some into the arms of their mamans if they were buried too, and some, we left curled, alone. We washed them sweet with roses, crocuses, and lilies of the valley.

—Even dried, those little flowers are useful, says Madelaine. —They do the job quickly, painlessly. A little oil, if fresh. Brewed, if dry, tea to the fevered lips of babies, too broken to fix . . .

—Too blue to breathe air, I finish.

Clémence closes her eyes. I can tell by the long breaths she takes that she is pulling in the smell of the flowers. She is learning to accept and to go on. That's good because she has a long way to go, this one.

no beginning

There are small cracks
webbed over the grief
of you leaving.

Tears gather
weight the web
threaten to expose the hole,
where you lived
so short a time.

There are mamans that kill babies,
I know. I know.
I blame myself
I've done something wrong.
Why else would you choose this maman to never have you?

The maman that kills babies.

x Rubis

Rivière-du-Renard, la Gaspé 1873

Rubis walks to the side of the house and begins to unpeg the washing. All of her son Raoul's clothes—three pants, four shirts, five pairs of socks, six underwear—have been washed, along with all the bedding. She stands for a moment, enjoying the sunshine, eyes closed. Her ears fill with wind, like crashing ocean waves, and sheets snapping for all the world like the sails on a tall ship. She opens her eyes. The movement of white sheets against the bright blue sky wakens something in her. She hears sibilant whispers inside her, all around her.

She sees ghost children and those not quite born run and laugh. The crops behind and above rise to the blood red sky, a familiar omen.

Rubis tingles when she recognizes her familiar woman, the one who always comes to her in this vision. She is dressed in the old style, small white bonnet covering her hair, heavy dark-blue skirt, and white shirt covered over with a long, white apron. She has no shoes. Her feet seem buried by or part of the blue stones that surround her. The two women stare at each other calmly. When they smile a flash of sunlight knifes through the mirrors of time. Rubis approaches her and stops when she can smell the woman. She is the scent of crocus and lily of the valley, the first flowers of spring.

Her cupped hands are filled with water. She pours it playfully over her own head. She smiles at Rubis through the water. She motions for Rubis to open her mouth. Rubis does so and tilts her head, closing her eyes to keep out the sky. She swallows and swallows but there is so much water. Rubis does not struggle, there is no point. She knows there is no end.

The sheets snap more loudly, the wind lowers its roar, and Rubis comes to herself, tangled in a wayward sheet still half-pegged to the line. She shakes her head slowly, to clear it of the vision. The taste of water is strong in her mouth, just like before.

She carefully unwinds herself from the sheet and unpegs the rest of the line. She puts the last peg in her apron pocket, stoops to pick up the basket, and falls to the ground sobbing. She has seen this drowning three times now. She knows what the woman is telling her.

The men are riding four abreast. They ride tall and easily, as if one with their horses. For the last fourteen hours they have ridden and eaten and slept with their mounts, which for these men is nothing new. They are Caillou men and through their veins runs the blood of ancient horsemen. Trainers, breeders, buyers, sellers, and everything in between.

Sometimes their wives wonder at this bond between man and horse, but they, like anyone who comes in contact with these people, never question it.

While stars still dotted the sky, while coyotes finished off their suppers, the men ate a hurried breakfast, packed up, and moved out in unison. Gilbert-Joseph takes the lead and Cléophase-Mathieu the tail-end, a two-year-old horse behind him.

It is a gift for Raoul, along with the tack and bridle. The boy will ride a long way and must prove himself horse-worthy, beyond what Rubis claims him capable of.

We'll see what the boy is made of, thinks Cléophase-Mathieu, chuckling to himself. Pierre-André glances over to his younger brother.

—What's so funny? he asks.

—Just wondering if Raoul can walk on water yet, laughs Cléophase-Mathieu.

Pierre-André smiles. —Probably can, if Rubis taught him.

—And does he still talk to birds? wonders Jean-Marc, the second oldest, out loud. —Imagine! He'll be able to tell us what we've been missing all these years!

—What do you mean, missing? scoffs Pierre-André. —I know what they say. They say: "Here's a tree, let's sit here. Here's some sky, let's fly. Oh! The wind, we can coast now. Look, there is the head of Jean-Marc, let's poop!"

—And look! barks Gilbert-Joseph good-naturedly. —There are four great lumps of manure who, if they don't move it, will never get anywhere! They will not have a soft bed to sleep in tonight and will have only wolves for singing partners! He tightens his knees to the horse's sides and slacks the reins, giving the horse his head.

The riders enter the yard singing "J'entends le moulin," the horses' hooves adding a syncopated rhythm. They see Rubis, laundry basket on her hip, Raoul, her son, tall, slight, and dark-haired, at her side. From this angle it is difficult to say who is supporting whom. One by one the brothers stop singing and dismount. The wind picks up and sweeps through the yard as the four men walk towards Rubis.

Gilbert-Joseph reaches her first. She passes the laundry to Raoul and allows herself to be enfolded by her brother's arms. She buries her face in his leather jacket. The others come forward and form a circle of arms and bodies and leather. They are all crying and Raoul tries not to stare. Then suddenly Cléophase-Mathieu grabs him and pulls him, basket and all, into the fray, and he finds himself sobbing. He feels like creek ice giving way in spring.

The dogs whine anxiously, smelling something, but unable to see it.

That night Raoul sits at the table surrounded by his mother's family. Pierre-André slips him a hard, black candy, —In case your mother's cooking hasn't improved! and his head is still reeling from the gift his uncle Cléophase-Mathieu has given him—a horse! Even now, above his mother's chattering and the noise of cutlery, his ears are tuned to the two-year-old in the barn.

—Raoul? Raoul, his mother says. —Eat your supper before it gets cold. Pierre-André, did you give him candy before supper? she asks, narrowing her eyes.

Pierre-André raises his hands in mock surrender. —Just a little licorice to help him digest! he explains.

—I still have it Mamie, see? Raoul opens his hand and reveals the candy. —I am saving it for later.

—An honest boy, very good Rubis! quips Jean-Marc dryly. —Now ask him if he'll eat it himself, or feed it to the horse out there.

—Oh non, mon oncle Jean-Marc! Not the horse, protests Raoul. —I don't think it would be good for him, he's too small and I . . . I don't know what it is, he finishes sheepishly.

—Excellent! booms Gilbert-Joseph. —I doubt you'll need it either Raoul. Rubis, this stew would make Jésus weep.

The brothers agree with him as they eat the rich stew with new vigour and butter still more slices of bread. Rubis is glad she remembered all her brothers' favourite foods: meat stew for Gilbert-Joseph, plenty of vegetables for Cléophase-Mathieu, bread with whole grains for Jean-Marc, and a jug of molasses for Pierre-André. With such a sweet tooth, one would expect him to be the size of a moose, but there he sits, lanky and lean.

Rubis gazes lovingly at her brothers. All over six feet tall, all muscle and great mops of hair, black to blonde and all shades in between. Gilbert-Joseph, she notices, has white peppered into his black. But it suits him, she thinks. Her gaze rests on Raoul, his face intent, his eyes watchful as he unconsciously mimics the older men's rhythm of eating, holding a piece of bread in the left hand to sop up the gravy.

Usually, she would insist on elbows off the table and other stiflings, but tonight she is free from that. She picks at her food, smiling, her eyes lighting on each in turn as he speaks or laughs. She gets up from her place and hurries to make more tea, cut more bread, get the jams and pies out, touching briefly each person at her table in passing, as if to reassure herself that they are indeed here and indeed real. She brings her hand to her throat often, feeling the pulse there, feeling the happiness slide like clean, cold water.

Finally the last of the stew, the bread, and the pies are eaten. Heavy, satisfied groans are chased down with the last cups of tea sweetened with honey. Gilbert-Joseph, Jean-Marc, Cléophase-Mathieu, and Raoul push back their chairs in unison after Gilbert-Joseph announces it's time to tuck in the horses.

—Kiss my lovely Léo for me, grunts Pierre-André. —I'll help Rubis wash up.

—Non, non, non, you go on, stretch your legs. I'll do the dishes, protests Rubis, slipping on her long apron.

Pierre-André grins ruefully.

—Could do with a bath, but I'll settle for suds up to my armpits.

The other men laugh and leave in a clatter of boot heels and whirl of coats.

Rubis pushes the hair off her forehead and leans over the sink to see out into the yard. Raoul walks solemnly with his uncles, leading the way with Cléophase-Mathieu, the two of them deep in conversation. She knows his stash of kittens will be appreciated.

—Thank you, Pierre-André, she whispers.

—Wait and see how many I break before you thank me, he growls, playfully brandishing a plate.

—Not the dishes, not just the dishes, for . . . the horse, for coming, for agreeing to take Raoul. Rubis hangs her head and cries into her apron.

He moves to take her in his arms.

—Too bad it's not spring, Pierre-André murmurs, —Flowers could do with all this water today, einh?

Her laughter muffled by the apron, she hiccups once and blows her nose, accepting the handkerchief he offers.

—It feels good to cry. It feels good to feel again. It's been a long time, Pierre-André, a long time.

—I know, little one, I know, he smoothes the hair on the top of her head with his big, wet hand. —You should have come back home after your Marc died. It's a damned hard life enough as it is, surrounded by family. You shouldn't have stayed here alone all this time without a husband.

He tilts her face towards his and dabs at her tears with his shirt-sleeve.

—Yes, she sighs, —it is a damned hard life sometimes. She leans against him briefly, feeling his heartbeat at her temple.

—It's not good, a woman here, on her own. Not safe, I don't like it one bit.

He begins to soap the dishes vigorously.

—Oh you! I've been here already twelve years. This is my home. People know me, neighbours depend on me. I love it here in my little house. I could never just leave . . .

She busies herself wiping the table.

—Why not? If it's the women you're thinking of, well, women had babies before you came here. Certainly they could squeeze out their runts without you holding their hand, he says, squeezing the wash cloth for emphasis.

—Pierre-André! It's not just the birthing; it's all the other work too! I'm needed here. These people need me.

—They may need you, but do you understand you shouldn't be alone? With Marc gone, it's dangerous, a woman on her own. You stick out, being so needed, so necessary, as you say. We've seen it at home, you know, those fucking priests! Always sticking their noses in our business. I think it's best to keep yourself to yourself these days. I think you should quit this place altogether and come with us.

He avoids her eyes.

—Don't start that again, please! It's not like home in Quatre-Pistoles. Here, we still help each other out. Why just the other day I helped out the neighbour, Trefflé, when he had an accident with his axe. Lucky he was so drunk, he hardly felt any pain at all. And his wife, Zoë, is expecting any day now. They have promised to deliver a winter's supply of wood after the baby is born. And they never once mentioned what l'Abbé said . . . she falters.

Pierre-André steals a glance at his sister.

—What did he say Rubis? What did l'Abbé ass-hole say?

21

—He said, "A man who puts himself on the equal with the Church, is a lost man." And I said, "We used l'eau de Pâques, Monsieur le curé," she says calmly.

Pierre-André closes his eyes, hands limp in the hot water.

—You what? he whispers.

—We used l'eau de Pâques, she repeats firmly. —For the cross, in the field. We did bless it, you know that. We did everything right. Just because we did not ask permission from the priest he says God made the wagon slip and crush Marc. I tried to stop the bleeding but it couldn't be done, I . . . I . . . it wouldn't stop. Maybe it doesn't work anymore, I don't know, she sighs heavily.

—Seigneur Jésus! Rubis, he says, opening his eyes, — It will only get worse. When Papa stopped finding water and couldn't stop the blood anymore, people became angry and afraid. They made his life a living hell. People like you and Papa, well, you want to help and you do good, but now you are making the priest mad. Then the rest of them become afraid. And then no matter what you do, if you still can do it, it's going to be wrong.

She puts her hand on his arm.

—I've ridden a horse before, Pierre-André, I know about balance, she says softly. —But I can't stop who I am. I can't stop what I know from happening.

—Non, of course not. But still . . . He pauses, uncertain.

—But still what?

—Well, still, you want Raoul away from here and I just think that proves that you should come with us too.

—Non, we've already decided this, she sighs wearily. —I stay here and Raoul goes with you. Raoul needs an education and he needs men in his life to teach him to be a man. And he's special, Pierre-André, and around here that . . .

—That means trouble right? he finishes for her.

–Not trouble exactly, just, well, just that . . . She is twisting her tea-towel into a rope as she speaks.

–He could be in trouble, right? persists Pierre-André.

–Oh you! she snaps him with the wet towel. –Enough of this! Let's leave it that he needs to be with family.

–Aren't you family? He holds her wrists so she can't turn from him. –Why won't you come with us Rubis?

She is saved from answering him by the sound of steps on the porch and the door banging open.

–Mamie! Mamie! Raoul shouts excitedly. –Look at what else they brought me! He carries a saddle into the kitchen and drops it on the table.

Rubis looks at her son then at each of her brothers in turn. Raoul notices that her eyes are oddly bright.

–Your own saddle, she whispers. –Now you can go. Now you are going.

She pulls the boy close and smells his good smell. He wraps his arms around her, breathing deeply to keep from crying.

The brothers stare at the wall, the ceiling, the crock-pot of beans ready for the oven, anywhere but the centre of the kitchen.

–We should sing, einh? Cléophase-Mathieu pipes up and pulls the mouth-organ from his breast-pocket.

"J'entends le moulin," floats through the air. Pierre-André and Gilbert-Joseph begin to sing with gusto while Jean-Marc plays the spoons, two pairs in each hand.

Rubis raises her head, conscious of her tears but unembarrassed. Raoul pulls away from her and in a gesture reminiscent of Pierre-André, wipes his mother's tears away with his shirt-sleeve. She smiles at him and they begin to dance, avoiding the shadows beyond the light.

Avant Talon

outside the trees dance bare

it's the dry time
when the wind comes flitting
and fighting from the hills
the heaving and the sighs

littered leaves make their escape
whirling the air with mute mouths

all things wild and forgotten
all things tossed and rotten
take centre-stage

for a reason

Frenchtown, Montana 1911

Raoul is dreaming of water. Ice-cold water in the month of October. He knows this because there are few leaves on the trees surrounding the pond. Is it a lake? No, smaller than a lake. It is very deep though, he can tell by the colour, dense blue, almost black. There is no bottom to this water.

Why is he near this water? This is the lake they call "La Chambre du Diable." It is maybe a mile from his old place in Gaspé.

Voices around him, coming from far away, are muffled, distorted. What do they say? Why are they angry? Are they shouting now, or getting closer?

He is bundled up against the cold. No, he is tightly bound. Heavy rope scratches at his wrists and ankles. The voices stop and he is floating.

Wait, he is sitting, sitting in a boat. He hears the sound of oars breaking the surface of the water, the creak of the lock as the oars are pulled. Suddenly, he is up and over, and all is reduced to cold water. It fills his eyes and mouth. Is he screaming? Are his eyes open or shut? One voice rages above him, muffled by water, by the distance between surface and depth.

He waits, suspended. He is so cold. Feels weight in his pockets, pulling him down. He looks up to where he imagines the surface is. He sees a dark face peering. He is wracked with cold again and sees nothing. Then, hair in front of his face, red hair that fades to blackness.

Beside him his wife, Marie-Irène, wakes up. Something is shaking the bed. She opens one eye and rolls to her left side. The shaking is coming from the bed itself. She rolls onto her back and puts her hand out to Raoul. He is shivering so hard his teeth rattle. She pulls herself to a sitting position, feels his forehead with the back of her hand. Jésus, Marie, and Joseph! He's burning! The pillow is soaked.

–Raoul? Raoul! Can you hear me? Are you awake? she whispers, gently shaking his shoulder.

She strokes his forehead and temple. He groans and mutters but is still deep in sleep.

She gets out of bed and lights the candle on the bedside table. Turning around to put on her housecoat, she catches a glimpse of Raoul's tousled black hair, damp and stringy wild. There are dark circles underneath his eyes; his skin has no colour save the slight shadow of his beard. His mouth is clamped shut as he groans. Legs curled up to his stomach and hands clutching the quilt, Raoul looks younger than his fifty-two years, more vulnerable, like a child, she thinks, an orphaned child.

She walks to the basin and pours water over the facecloth. Wringing it well, she folds it expertly and gently touches his face and neck. She flips the cloth over and leaves it on his forehead.

She straightens and tightens the belt of her robe. Right, she thinks, he is still sleeping. She glances at the window, sees the crescent moon in the upper right-hand pane. Still late. I'll get the camomile tea and some willow bark ready. He will have one of his headaches in the morning. Pray the fever breaks by breakfast.

She kisses two fingers and lays them on the side of his neck. He is wracked by another shiver. The quilt seems alive. She hurries from the room into the dark kitchen.

He dreams of climbing the hill that gives way to the west pasture. The air smells of water, rain, and pond. He climbs steadily and easily, relishing the pull and flex of his muscles.

He reaches the crest of the hill and stands looking down over his land. He sees the ranch that he and his uncles have built up over the last forty-odd years, stretching to the west and up into the mountains. Soft, yellow fields of wheat and hay give way to pasture, redolent with sweet clover and buffalo grass. Horses and cattle dot the hillsides.

Philia, his seventh child, rides up, flanked by her brothers Patrique and Léo. Behind them in fan formation are five children, also on horseback.

One has streaks of blood where her eyes should be; she is plump and smiling into the mist, as though listening to a pleasant conversation. Beside her is one with no ears, dressed all in blue and carrying water on her shoulders. Her long hair ripples and stains red in places. The next child he sees is winged, like a dragonfly, and her head swivels like an owl. When she sees Raoul, she waves. Her hand sprays the northern lights. The one beside Philia has something wrong with her foot; it is twice as large as the other one. Raoul feels relief that this one has the strongest, darkest horse carrying her, so she will not have to walk. Something winks in this girl's hand. It is his small silver scythe, the one he uses to cut leather strips. The last one rides with a thundercloud for a cloak. Her reins are made of small, highly polished bones that tinkle hollowly. Around her neck he sees the blue rosary. She is singing in a low, throaty voice the song his mother used to sing to him when he was a child:

> C'est le matin et le
> soleil se lève et le
> dos de la lune scintille.
>
> Tous les oiseaux,
> sont encore au berceau.
> L'eau et le vent se gazouillent.
>
> C'est le soupire de Dieu,
> c'est le sourire de Dieu,
> c'est la promesse du Bon Dieu.

Raoul is happy. They are singing and it sounds like his mother's voice. He hasn't heard Rubis's voice for so long. He smiles and Marie-Irène can hear him laugh out loud.

–Silly old man, she mutters to the kettle. –I married a sad little boy who grew up to be a silly old man.

She hums to herself as she mixes up the headache powder, following the recipe in Rubis's book.

In the morning he has one of his headaches; she can tell by the far away look in his eyes and the careful measure of his words. Raoul refuses to stay in bed, however. He is up, shaved, and sitting at the table, thumbing through the catalogue when Marie-Irène comes in from her morning chores.

–Paul-Émile, Bella-Rose, Annie-Béatrice, 'Ti Paul, Patrique, Léo, Philia, Claude-André, Émérentienne-Marguerite; he repeats his children's names like a litany, like a prayer, their names rolling off his tongue with pleasure.

–What are you doing, old man? Buying me a present for being such a good wife? she chuckles.

–Saddles, he mutters without looking up, –the children will need saddles.

–Saddles? What children? Annie's three already have them, and . . .

–Patrique and Léo's children need saddles, he says matter-of-factly. –Or maybe girls would rather those gauntlets with the fringe and beadwork.

–Patrique and Léo have no children, she tut-tuts, throwing more of the herbs into the teapot and putting the kettle on to boil.

Raoul lowers the catalogue carefully and looks into her face. She notices that his eyes are strangely bright. The headache does that, she thinks.

–But they will have children, petit Jésus, they most certainly will, he whispers almost fiercely.

A shiver passes through her.

–What are you talking about? she asks softly, moving the frying pan to a hot part of the stove.

—Marie-Irène, I saw angel children in my dreams. Twins, no less! One set each, girls!

—Twin girls? Both Patrique and Léo? My, my, that fever really did show you a few things, didn't she? And did she also tell you that Philia and Delphis will be here tonight? We have to get them rigged up for the trip to Alberta, remember? Marie-Irène flicks a few drops of water into the frying pan, to see if it is hot enough.

—Yes, yes, he says impatiently. We will have the rest of the week to get them organized. Delphis, Monsieur Smart Man, he has everything planned, and Philia has been packing since they got that letter from the church. If they had just bought that land before Coteau got a hold of it, we'd be all set . . . he says as angrily as his throbbing head will allow.

—Raoul mon vieux, calm down. There's nothing to do about that now, except to make sure they are well provided for until they get to that Alberta, einh?

She flops bacon strips into the frying pan.

Raoul stares morosely at the front door, tracing the figure eight over and over again on the oilcloth.

—Raoul? Why don't you go lie down for a while? Marie-Irène suggests kindly. —The boys can take your chores today. You need to rest. You had a bad night last night.

She busies herself with the teapot and hot water.

—Chère Mère Marie-Irène, I thank you for your concern. However, there is work to be done. I can rest plenty long enough once I'm dead. Thank you very much quand même.

He smiles but does not get up from the table.

Marie-Irène places a cup of the headache infusion in front of him. She lays a hand on his neck and gently rubs the knots there. She sighs and turns to tend to the bacon.

Raoul sips the brew and returns to his catalogue. Everything in his experience prepares him for the inevitable parting with his child, Philia, but he does not accept it easily. All his life, it seems, he has been saying goodbye, to his father when he was eleven, his mother when he was thirteen. Gilbert-Joseph and his beloved comrade Pierre-André both died in the winter of his twentieth year. Then, at thirty, to lose his two youngest children to the church, one to the nunnery in Missoula and the other to the priesthood, the Oblates in Montréal, for all the sense that makes!

—Why can't people just stay put? he wonders out loud.

—What's that? asks Marie-Irène.

—Nothing, nothing, just talking to myself is all. I think I'll go check the horses.

—What? Breakfast is almost on the table.

—I'm not hungry this morning, he mumbles, slurping down the rest of his tea.

He stands and stretches.

—Wait just one minute, Monsieur, scolds Marie-Irène. —You need something in that gut of yours besides worry. Here, she hands him a bacon sandwich, —take this with you and eat it all. The dogs don't need bacon.

—Merci ma belle.

He takes the sandwich and bites into it to reassure her.

—Be back before dinner?

He walks out the door into the bright morning sunshine. He waves at her from behind his back to show that he has heard. He is just too tired to speak.

Marie-Irène sighs heavily and watches her husband walk slowly across the yard. She slumps down in her rocking chair.

She too worries about Philia going away. She knows that Patrique and Léo will accompany them. A woman knows, she thinks, a woman knows that the minute your child leaves your body, he begins to leave you forever. A man doesn't accept that the child is leaving until the wagon leaves the yard. It always hits men harder.

She touches her face. Every child she has carried, accounted for: there, in the lines of her face, even the ones she has lost. A woman cannot, ever, forget her children.

Raoul looks up at his favourite horse. He winks at him and the horse snickers delightedly. He ambles over to Raoul and they make little hello noises to each other.

—Einh mon vieux, einh? I am needing you today my old friend. Take me upon your back and bring me to where I am young again, einh? Can you take me there? Can you? Yes, of course you can. Let's you and me go now.

He leaps upon the horse's back and rides bareback. Smelling the horse, relishing in the animal's steadfast company as he always has, he rides head-long into his past.

This morning brings news of a horse in trouble. I took Raoul with me because Marc was already in the field.

When we got to Têtrault's farm the horse was lying down in the warm sun-shine, snuffling and snorting and terribly confused. Raoul understood what to do right away.

—Maman, he doesn't know why his leg doesn't work. He is very worried about that. I will help him and you fix the leg.

It is because we have played out this scene at our place—birds, kittens, dogs, weasels with their little bones broken for one reason or another—that Raoul has a sense of purpose and is determined to help. He is like my father and can speak to animals.

From the side, he walks right up to the head of the horse, stepping delicately

32

over desperately churning legs and heavy hooves. He bends right over the horse's face and begins his little hello noises, breathing into the horse as I taught him and using only his forehead to touch, no arms swinging around, no hands causing more confusion. The horse takes only a moment to register this little being, then calms down, sides heaving with relief at being heard.

It's not a particularly bad break, very clean really, and easily mended. I check for bone splinters, wash out the break with l'eau bénit, realign the bones, and sew him up while they begin to assemble what will be needed for the plaster.

—Monsieur would like some oats and honey, warmed, please, nickers Raoul very softly.

—What? What the hell did he say? Têtrault barks.

—I believe the horse would like some oats and honey, warmed please, I say, looking past the man and smiling at my son.

—What the hell is this? Christly kid talks to horses now, does he? Têtrault smirks.

—Child of Christ indeed, Monsieur, and I would listen to him if you ever want another day's work out of this beast, I reply, going back to my sewing.

The horse chuffs in agreement. Raoul coos and rubs his forehead between the giant's eyes. The horse groans with pleasure and settles more heavily onto the ground.

Monsieur Têtrault laughs out loud. —Don't you mess up that horse, Raoul! I need him to work hard, soon!

—Not too soon, I caution, cutting the thread with my teeth. —He will need about four or five weeks before the break is mended. In the meantime . . . oats and honey are perfect. Warmed, please. It will keep him from going into shock, I say, straightening up and dusting my skirt.

—Mamie? I will stay with him for a while and see that he is happy. Then I will come home, Raoul says, finally using his hands to stroke the horse's neck.

—Yes, that's good, I nod. —Monsieur? Have you any objections? Will there be someone to see him home safely? I ask the owner, nodding toward Raoul.

—How can I say non? The boy will lay some sort of curse on the horse if we separate them now, I suppose . . . Têtrault sniffs wetly.

—It is no curse that Raoul knows. He would never hurt your horse. He wants it to be happy is all. He understands animals, Monsieur, I say firmly. —I want no confusion about this, Raoul will be coming with me from now on when I have animals to work with, and there must be no fear on your part.

—What the hell are you on about? Têtrault snaps. —I would make a bargain with the devil himself to keep from having to shoot that horse. We really need . . .

—To trust more in God and what is good than to make bargains with the devil, Monsieur, I finish, crossing myself.

—Yes, yes, of course, trust in God, he mumbles quickly, crossing himself. —Lucien! he calls to his son gawking from the fence. —Get some mash ready for the horse, use warm water. And get some honey from the house to sweeten it, he finishes, staring hard at Raoul.

Raoul smiles, lays his head on the horse's neck, and closes his eyes.

His work is just beginning, I think as I walk home. And he is but six years old. My father would be proud of him.

Raoul is thinking, I can hear this baby. He is tired and scared. I will stay here and feed him the food that Mamie gives me when I am scared. Mamie makes me bread and cream and sugar, nice and thick. This baby needs that too, but not milk, I think. He is too big for that. Something sweet between his teeth will feel good.

When Raoul gets up the horse rises, albeit gingerly. He follows the little dark-haired boy to the barn, where he trusts the food will be.

▨ The outskirts of Québec City 1873

Raoul has been wearing the same underwear for seven days now. The excitement of travelling with his own horse and sleeping under the stars has made him forget everything else. After enduring Pierre-André's none-too-gentle chiding at supper, he has washed himself as best he can in the dish-water and now he searches for a clean pair of socks and underwear. It is important to look his best tomorrow, well, at least not to smell too badly.

His uncles have made plans to meet the others who will be travelling with them to Mont Ana, this Frenchtown place. There are supplies to be bought, maps and guides to consult, and the cardinal from Québec to bless their voyage. All very exciting, all terribly confusing. He doesn't want to seem the country idiot his uncles tease him about being. Raoul digs deeper into the leather bag that holds all his possessions.

His hand touches the hard shape of something lodged in the dark recesses of the bag. He pulls out a small, flat red book. He smiles. Maman's little book! She always said it was for him—her stories, her drawings, and her special recipes. He frowns. He isn't supposed to read it until the day of his wedding. Well, she gave it to me now, he thinks, so I'll read just a few parts and save the rest for later.

The search for underwear forgotten, he brings the book over to his uncles who are sitting around the fire.

–What's that there, boy? drawls Jean-Marc, shifting a log with the toe of his boot.

–A book, says Raoul settling himself next to Cléophase. –Mamie's book.

–A fairy-tale book is it? laughs Gilbert-Joseph. –Rubis was ever the one for stories, einh? Why don't you read one to us?

–I don't think they are fairy-tales, hesitates Raoul. –She used this book to draw the flowers she picked for medicine, and she wrote about things that happened when I was young, too young to remember. She said it was so that I would know what it was like before, before . . . he stops suddenly.

Pierre-André narrows his eyes and speaks softly. –Before your father died? he asks.

–Yes, I guess, sighs Raoul.

—Well, that's a good thing, to remember your father, I mean, Gilbert-Joseph says gruffly.

—Yes, whispers Raoul, touching the book's cover tenderly.

Pitiful thing, thinks Jean-Marc. Rubis is wrong to send him away with us. He should have stayed with her, or at least she should have come with us. To lose his father in the last year is one thing, but this, this leaving is like losing his mother too.

He kicks at the log with more force than necessary, sending up sparks and illuminating Raoul's tear-stained face.

Cléophase-Mathieu throws his arm around Raoul. —Hey, come on now. Why don't you read some of it and then we'll tell you the real story, einh? Your Mamie was so in love with that crazy half-breed father of yours that she probably has him shining like Jésus Himself in those stories there, he taps the cover of Rubis's book. —I want to see if she said anything about the time he was caught swimming naked in the pond out by your place by l'Abbé, on a Sunday morning no less! he laughs good-naturedly, nudging Raoul.

Raoul laughs shakily and wipes his eyes with the sleeve of his shirt. —Yes, she told me about that. And about the time you and Papa rode the pigs into town . . .

—What? She told you about? That was not my idea, protests Cléophase. It was Jean-Marc who thought we should try it. He winks at his brother.

But Jean-Marc doesn't reply. He stares into the flames.

Pierre-André chuckles and shakes his head. —Read some of it to us, will you Raoul? I'd like to have some of those memories refreshed.

He stretches his long legs towards the fire and settles back against his sleeping roll.

Raoul smiles, licks his top lip, and bends the book open towards the fire-light. He reads what Rubis has written on the inside cover, her elegant handwriting captured in dark-blue, almost-black ink:

Asleep on stones

dusty shadow sage
twist of bone somewhere
there asleep on stones

smoothed by ghost snow
cradled in the arms of ghost water
asleep on stones
lovely lullaby still
winds kiss quietly and completely
ravens keep watch

I am not a very old woman. I will never be, I know this. I am thirty years old.
Today is my birthday and I watched you ride off to a new life.

My life has taken me from my father's house in beautiful Quatre-Pistoles, le
talon de la Gaspé, to here, where I lived with your father in beautiful Rivière-
du-Renard. I pray your life takes you to a beautiful place too. I love you, my
Raoul, be happy.

Your loving maman, Rubis

The men shift slightly. They had not expected this, so much like Rubis, as if
she is there among them, speaking the words out loud.

Pierre-André clears his throat. –Read something else. Find a funny part
maybe, einh?

Raoul flips to the first page. He reads—

My name is Rubis Marie-Victoire Caillou Morin. Marc, Monsieur Marc Joseph
Morin, that's my husband's name. I like the sound of that, my husband. We
were married three weeks ago. It feels like we've always been married.

When I first heard his voice something inside me woke up and I felt that my
life was just beginning. I think he felt that way too, though he swears it was my
breasts that he fell in love with. Men! You can't get them to think with the big

*head sometimes. I know he says that just to make me laugh. That's how I know
I love him, he makes me laugh.*

x Rubis

Jean-Marc stands up and yawns dramatically. —Well, if that's as funny as it
gets, I'm going to bed. I listened for fourteen years to that sort of stuff from
Rubis, so I think I know the rest. Good night to you all.

The others laugh and follow his lead. They begin pulling out tarps and
bedrolls.

Raoul smiles. This is a good present, he thinks. I will read a little every
night. It will be like hearing her voice again. A shiver passes through him
and the hair on his arms stands up. Automatically, he crosses himself.

Raoul crawls in beside Cléophase, under the tarp. Fighting an overwhelm-
ing desire to cry, he keeps his eyes wide open and watches the stars, knowing that his mother needs him awake tonight. Needs him to watch.

Rivière-du-Renard, Gaspé décembre 1873

Pulchérie Trefflé:

I'll do it. I will go where he wants to go. Do anything to keep
the world from going black.

This place is dangerous.
The men don't listen to us anymore.

People want to know—
    Where is Madame Rubis? Have you seen Rubis Morin?
    They ask me, like I know something they don't.

They look at us and
they know
about all that.

They know what happened that night.

So
we have to leave.

Antoine Trefflé:

There are too many people here.
Watchin' me all the time.
Place is too small now.

Télèsphore had it all,
biggest share of land around here. Zoë's father gave him a whole section
after they got married . . .
Good land, good water on the land, everything.

He could of married another one, her sister maybe even.
Crazy bâtard, why bother the healer woman?
Why mess with that Morin woman?

I swear to God, his craziness will infect us all.

So we go ouest,
me and la bonne femme and Baptiste

Get away from this place.
Forget the craziness.

It can't follow us.

Antoine pulls out his pipe, scrapes it clean, and as he fills it with tobacco,
he begins to sing,

> Un Canadien errant,
> Bani de ses foyers,
> Un Canadien errant,
> Bani de ses foyers,
> Parcourait en pleurant

Des pays étrangers
Parcourait en pleurant
Des pays étrangers.

Un jour, triste et pensif,
Assis au bord des flots,
Un jour triste et pensif,
Assis au bord des flots,
Au courant fugitif
Il adressa ces mots:

"Si tu vois mon pays,
Mon pays malheureux,
Si tu vois mon pays,
Mon pays malheureux,
Va,
dis à mes amis
Que je me souviens d'eux,

Va,
dis à mes amis
Que je me souviens
d'eux."

Delphis Massie:

Bastards, the English will take over every square inch of the new land if we
    let 'em.
Then were will we be?
No good Catholics around
no good nothing.

Philia knows
she knows why we go.
She was sitting right there beside the old man Raoul when Monseigneur
    told us about the duty we have
to protect our language
to preserve our Church
to keep out the English
to, to, to . . .
Me?

What the Christ do I care about all that?
I need land.
Being the youngest, there was nothing left for me in Québec
and I'll be goddamned if I let this opportunity pass me by!
A man is nothing without land, some inheritance for his kids.
His own place, where a man can grow old in peace.

Break a family so that a people can survive,
I don't give a damn.
Whatever it takes
I'll do.

Delphis and Philia (Morin) Massie:

—You are going too fast Delphis! We most certainly need clothes! Here, put
that in the trunk.

—We need a pot to piss in, that's all.

—What about the tools?

—Fuck the tools. All the farm stuff is your father's, it stays here. I need my tongs and hammer and the anvil. Maybe a few shoes, nails, and my gun . . .

—But to farm?

—The devil take the tools! And while he's at 'er, give 'im the farm too! Let's just go, la petite. You and me. Your brothers, Patrique and Léo. We'll find out what it means to be maître chez-nous. Chez nous! There's nothing left for us here anyway.

She thinks—I'll wrap the teacups that his mother gave us as a wedding present, and these small glasses too. They go here, inside the pot he mended. I'll have to make sure to have steel wool and the lye soap. The headache powder, where is my headache powder? I'll have to get more from Papa before I leave.

He thinks—Family? We'll be family. We will start again. Family don't need us, Montana can't have us.

Talon

[   ] A copy of the Dominion's Land Act of 1872.

First year, living no further than 2 miles from the intended homestead, clearing 10 acres and assuring that 5 of those acres are able to support crops. Second year, seeding those 10 acres and clearing 15 others. Third year, seeding those 25 acres and clearing 12 more. Build a house and live in it for three months preceding your request for official registration of lands.

Alternative/Folk Medicine / Part 1

Course: Physiology and Human Anatomy—Doctor Bussière

Interview with: Philia Marie Morin Massie
Location: Talon, Alberta
Date: April 1961
Interviewer: Phélice Trefflé

Philia: This box records my voice? Is it on now? Allo? Allo? Oh. What? Oh, yes, okay. Well, look at your mom over there. Léonie, my own daughter, clucking her tongue at me. She clucks her tongue at her own mother! She doesn't want me to talk to you, Phélice, to tell you the stories. Thinks I'm too old now. That I've forgotten them. Maybe you'd like to talk to someone else instead, einh?

Einh, Léonie? Or did you forget too? Like you can make a thing disappear just because you don't talk about it anymore. Or maybe you should talk to Clémence, sitting there, mute like stone. Do you want to tell a story Clémence? Tell your god-daughter a story about a monster?

Bah! You two should have been less afraid and more smart when the monsters were alive. Pathetic to be afraid of dead men. They do their best work when they are alive, I say.

What? Oh, well yes, alright yes, some are nasty in death too, but nothing we can't handle, einh? What? What was that? Oui, did you say? Did you say oui? Speak up girl! I can't hear you.

That's what I thought you said. Hmmph, that's better. Ah well, Baptiste was crazy anyways, that one. Said he heard voices of all things, like Joan of bloody Arc! And Reuville, well, no one can explain everything anymore.

I guess it's better that way, for some people, einh? Nice and clean and gone . . .

Too much talking and people start thinking you are the Devil or worse, a prophet, einh? And we all know what happens to them, we know, don't we Léonie? (She chuckles.) You end up like the Little One up there. (She points to the cross over the kitchen door) He heard voices too . . .

Oh stop rolling your eyes at me Léonie! If the wind changes, your face'll stay like that. You, a mother and still acting like a spoiled gamin. Pathetic.

Go ahead Phélice, ask me anything. Vas-y fille.

Phélice: Let's start with some background. I will ask you about some of the healing and medicines you used in a bit. Let's just get warmed up.

How do you feel, being a member of a minority? A French ship on an English ocean so to speak?

Philia: A what? Come again? Minorité? That's when there's not too many of you, right? We weren't a minorité, there was just us. You must mean women, we had lots of boys in those days. Only thing we had more of than boys was rocks. Some big as men and as stubborn, einh? Ever try changing the ideas of a man? Like pulling rocks, let me tell you! You have to pull and pull and dig around them and keep pulling. Mostly end up with a pain somewhere, you know? I remember one time when . . . ah, what was the question? Stupid question, never mind. Ask me something else. Ask me the stuff we talked about before.

Phélice: Are you a healer?

Philia: Well, a ramencheur—a fixer—mostly. Healer sounds like a whole other business. I did the bones and the fire and other people here did other things.

Phélice: You did the fire? What do you mean by that?

Philia: Fire, like a burn. I take the fire out of a burn so it won't blister or scar.

Phélice: How do you do that?

Philia: I don't do it, God does. You know that.

Phélice: What I meant was, are there special things you do, to help God? Special plants, prayers perhaps?

Philia: Prayers! Prayers like, like I was taught of course.

Phélice: (sigh) Can you recite those prayers for me now?

Philia: Do you have a burn?

Phélice: No, but I—

Philia: Then I won't say them. You think you could just write the prayer and you could do it too, einh? I tell you, it's not like that. It's from your blood. Shame on you Phélice! You were raised better than that. Raise the sleeve on your shirt ma fille and tell me you can tell where the fire kissed you. Tell me you stopped that fire yourself, einh? Tell me who did.

Phélice: You stopped the fire, Mémère. I know that, Mom knows that, ma tante Clémence knows that. I want other people to know too, that's all. The prayers, I could write them down, so people would know.

Philia: Don't be stupid. Who do you think wants to know this? No one asks for help anymore. They can all go to hell for all I care. Qu'le diable les prends. All run to doctors, wait in shitty hospitals for someone to poke you with a dirty needle or pop a pill in your mouth to shut you up. Can't get better in a hospital, surrounded by sick and germs. Your pépère Delphis, he died in a hospital.

Phélice: Please Mémère, you agreed to do this interview. I need your prayers for my research. Remember? The course with that nice Doctor Bussière? Where we can document the work you did, and others too, before doctors came to Alberta. And you don't want the prayers to be lost do you? I need to write them down, you would be helping me.

Philia: Phélice Trefflé, you stop this right now. Nothing is lost, not now, not ever. Prayers go where they should go. Nothing is lost. It is you, the lost thing. You give me a headache with all your fancy questions and fancy 'tate regorder'.

You want prayers? I'll give you prayers. Pray you are never on the wrong side of God. You want stories? I'll give you stories. Tell you about things that went on in this place. Tell you about the will of God and the people He chose to do His will.

Léonie! Get my book. Yes, you know damned well where it is, Madame Snoopy looking at it just the other day. Under the Vièrge in my room. Go.

Clémence, call over to Léo's. Marie is over there today helping with the cleaning, so she can drive him over, no excuses this time. And call Patrique, let's get this done right.

Phélice, I'm making some tea now and when the others get here, we are going to talk. You can hear all about it from those who were there, those who were chosen to do God's work. Listen and learn little one, listen and learn. This is your inheritance.

Philia broods in silence. Thinks,

it's like the end of a Wednesday rope
people expect you to do it
because you can
never a please
just a list of complaints
fix this, fix that,
then they go away

don't admire your house or garden
don't ask about your limp
or comment on the dark circles round your eyes

don't see you really
as a person

some, like Baptiste Trefflé,
turn to the black side of their gift

47

ignoring the silver side of the mirror
ignoring their responsibility
and that
leads to trouble

we have to stop this trouble once and for all
but where to start and what to tell?
Phélice wants to know about the gifts, that's the easy part
about Reuville and Léonie though, that'll bring in all of us
Morin, Massie, Trefflé, Casavant, Beaupré

Ah, she looks like so much like me, like Rubis, maybe she is strong enough
maybe she is the one to do this
we don't have much time
there's so much to say
where to start?

▦ Talon 1928

Dogs barking. Philia gets up from the table, leaves her coffee cup there
and goes to the window facing the front yard. Amidst the dust and
dappled shadows, a shape solidifies. It is very small, with four legs, leads
with the left shoulder as if walking through a storm. She sees now, as the
crows and magpies begin their litany of the world's ills, that two of those
legs are crutches and the child, for that is what it is, is dragging his right
leg.

She rubs her temples with both hands. A man, very tall and muscular, a
woman, and four other children emerge from a vehicle. The woman has a
baby in her arms. A sharp word, a turn of her head, and the children scatter.
Only the man steps to keep up with the child on crutches; the mother leans
against the vehicle.

At the porch steps the man removes his hat. Says something to the boy and
mounts the steps one at a time. He knocks on the door. The space between
heartbeats. Between eye and mouth.

Philia opens the inner wooden door and stands there, framed by the screen door.

—Yes?

—Bonjour Madame. My name is Baptiste Trefflé. I'm looking for Madame Philia Massie. My son, he gestures with his hat, —my son Philip needs some attention.

Philia automatically stiffens at the name. —Where are you from, Monsieur? she asks.

—We're from Autant, Madame. You know the place?

—Yes, yes, says Philia, briskly rubbing the goose-bumps on her arms. —I know the place well enough. You have family around here?

—Well now, that depends. We just moved to Talon and I don't know every-one in these parts, he smiles crookedly.

Philia looks him deep in the eyes. He does not turn away. There are more goose-bumps prickling her scalp. She sighs wearily. —I am Philia Massie. Show me the leg.

The man gestures for the boy to undress. —Enlèves tes culottes.

The boy struggles with the crutches and fumbles with the knot on his overalls.

—Non, non, non! Not outside! Inside, inside. Come on, be quick, she snaps, turning from the door.

The man holds out his hand to the woman beside the vehicle. She shakes her head no and returns to the vehicle with her fussing baby. She begins the business of feeding this one. The man gives a small shrug and rubs a hand over his stubbled jaw. Philia sees he carries the weight of days and years deep inside him. They make up his substance.

Man and boy meet on the top stair, the screen door croaks importantly, and they cross the threshold.

Philia watches while the woman stretches herself out on the long seat of the truck. She wears her life heavily, on top of herself, so that at any moment she might shrug and let everything slide from her shoulders, back, and heart. At any moment she could shake her skirts and the children and the man would fall from her like so much sawdust. She looks forty, but, Trefflé women age quickly.

Philia shrugs her shoulders then rounds on the two males.

—Well, don't stand there all owl-eyed, come in, come in. Take off your boots. Were you born in a barn? And you, she juts her chin towards the boy, —take your pants off, here, near the window. I need the light.

The boy moves quickly but stiffly. Clumsily propping the willow-branch crutches against the window frame, he fumbles with the knot holding the strap and his pants together. He moves to the other side and awkwardly unclasps the hook there. Philia knows he is used to opening his pants from the other side; the knot is new. The overalls fall to the floor.

He wears a threadbare undershirt and no underwear. She automatically counts the ribs heaving through the fabric, like rings on a tree, and resists the old impulse to pry open his mouth and count his teeth. She sees the bruise blooming from his hip, blood purple, up his side to the third rib, and down past the knee, already tinged yellow. A fresh hurt, not more than a month old. The hip is a misshapen lump of bone and muscle. She can feel the heat from there. She clucks her tongue as she hitches up her skirts to squat behind him. The bruise goes to his buttock.

—What in holy hell happened? She touches the small of his back to prompt him.

The father narrows his eyes at the touch.

—A horse stepped on him, Baptiste says loudly. Briskly, he continues, —The horse got spooked and knocked him over and then stepped on him. It was an accident, really.

—Lucky he stepped on the hip. It would have broken the back for sure, Philia mutters, getting up.

The boy determinedly bites his lip.

—Easy, little one, easy there now boy. Philia cups his face. She feels him trembling.

—Maybe he's hungry, says Trefflé. We haven't eaten today. Maybe a little egg or milk or something?

—He'll just puke it up. This is going to hurt. You can feed him after. I need you here, she says, looking into Philip's eyes, —on the table. You, Baptiste Trefflé, help him up, and I'll need you to hold him down.

—You can fix this? whispers Phillip weakly.

—God willing, yes. Now up you go. Come on.

She removes the honey bowl, the jar of spoons, and her coffee cup from the table. The boy heaves himself up and lies flat on the table, grimacing with pain. Philia begins the prayers for strength, for help, that she learned from her father. She holds the boy's foot and slowly moves the leg up and down. A feeling of nausea washes through her. She focuses her eyes on his hip. The boy softly whimpers. The nausea knots and roils in her stomach.

—M Trefflé, hold him down. No matter what happens. From the chest down, he must not move.

Baptiste nods, positions himself, and pins the boy down. She grasps the leg below and above the knee. Her fingers and hands seem to disappear into the bruise. The nausea threatens to boil over. The veins in her arms billow and pump. She mutters the prayer, clenches her teeth, and waits, waits, all the while increasing the pulling pressure. The boy's eyes grow wide and his throat cords with unsung screams.

Slowly she pulls and twists. The sound of bees travels from her head into her arms, hands, and fingers. Pull, pull, pull. The boy erupts in screams that shake the muscles in his hip loose. The nausea brims, threatens her mouth, sweat drips from her head. She has closed her eyes and now goes by feel alone. Bone is wrenched over bloated tissue and the bruising gives way to bone coming home. Shattered pelvis pieces knit together under the assault of prayer and power.

The boy turns his head to one side and pukes. Another release and the give of more muscle ripped open again to allow . . . There! There! Stop there. Done.

In her head the sound of bees and light, the smell of vomit, and the flapping tail-ends of finished prayers.

She looks at the leg. Her hands have left new, vivid prints on the boy. He retches again, spitting threads of thin, green bile from his lips.

She backs away and sits heavily on a straight-backed chair, finishing the prayer. Baptiste loses his grip on the boy.

A magpie coughs from the willow tree. Sparrows silver the air with bells. A small, cool wind wisps through the smell and light of the kitchen.

Philia raises her head and looks at the boy, now unconcious on the table. Blood drums in her throat, the light fades off to the left. The sound of bees lessens. Her arms begin to cool and her hands regain their natural colour.

–Madame? Madame? Baptiste Trefflé edges away from the table. –Is it . . . is he . . . the boy? He is done? Madame?

–He needs to sleep, she says thickly. –My neighbour will help now.

–Your neighbour, Madame? Where is she? Shall I go get her?

–M Trefflé, my neighbour, Madame Corneille.

Madelaine lifts her chin in the direction of a tall, female figure, at that moment moving from the porch into the kitchen.

–Madame Corneille, this is M Baptiste Trefflé and his son Philip.

With each clipped word Philia is banishing the bees and the heat. She stands, a steady hand smoothing her hair.

–Philip needs to sleep. I think the back room will be cool enough today. Will you help me move him and bind the hip? Non, non, M Trefflé, you've done enough. Go to your wife and tell her everything is all right. We'll clean him up and make sure he's comfortable.

The slender, dark-skinned neighbour wipes up the vomit, fills the kettle and sets it to boil on the stove, never once acknowledging the man's presence. Together, the women turn the boy gently away from the injured hip, lift and carry him between them into the shadow of the back room.

Once the women have turned their backs to him, Baptiste allows his anxious face to relax. The boy knew better than to say anything, but being half out of his head in pain, well, you never know what could have slipped out. So that's done then, he thinks.

Evelyn was right, these women know what they are doing. And now, of course, how to pay.

I always charge for the service I provide. To stop the fire in a burn is a great thing and those I heal are always more than generous, anxious as they are to stay on my good side. It's a pity that I couldn't fix the boy's leg, but it is always unwise to try to heal your own flesh and blood. Too bad, could have saved myself the price of this. This woman, this Philia Massie, he muses, what will she ask of me in return?

His thoughts are interrupted by the high-pitched wailing of his newest son, Urbain. Evelyn, he thinks, I must tell her about the boy. He grunts, finds his hat on the counter, and leaves the kitchen. The screen door protests as the kettle begins to hiss and squeal.

Philip Trefflé lies in the cool back room of Philia's house. He does not hear her come in. He does not smell the rose-water she bathes his face and hands and feet with. Does not feel the brush in his hair or hear the whispered prayers. He is doing his own work. He is dreaming himself through to the other side.

Since the accident his dreams are filled with horses of fire, with sharp steel hooves, menacing and chasing him through thorns of such pain that he wakes sweating and trembling. A scream is caught, just barely caught in his hands as he retches air, bile, and whatever little supper he had eaten onto the floor.

When the dream begins on this day, he finds himself in the barn at the farm in Autant. He leads the horse and smells the hay from its breath on his hair. He knows he will have to face his father soon, he always does. He begins to shake. Feels the lead begin to tighten. Hears the pawing of hooves and the snort of the horse. Philip tries to not be afraid; the waves of fear transmit too easily to the horse. He tries to slow his breathing.

A small blue light catches his eye. It is still far away. He watches it draw nearer and nearer. The horse shies sideways, lifting its enormous hooves, uncertain of the ground.

Philip welcomes this light. There has never been light before. He knows the horse is anxious, but it feels more normal now; it is something he too can see and he is less afraid.

And something else . . . what is this? Over the usual rank smell of urine and animal sweat shed in panic there is the perfume of roses! Philip clings to these new objects in his dream, holds them tight to his eyes, his heart. They comfort him.

Baptiste Trefflé looms. With a roar he slaps down hard and the rose scent is cut into small whispers. He swings both hands up and out through the light, trying to beat it down. The light breaks in two, becomes two eyes, lights from a face.

Clémence?

Non, non, non!

Baptiste kneels over her, pinning her to the ground. She opens her mouth. Baptiste's jams, she swallows and swallows and swallows. Shuddering, gagging noises coming from her whole body.

The scent of roses becomes wide and whole again. Baptiste's penis breaks off from his body.

Blue light pours from his crotch. He stumbles away from Clémence and pulls desperately at his own skin, trying to stop the light. It is dissolving him as surely as lye on skin. He is reduced to stumps, becomes skeletal. His face melts, mouth long and drawn out, lop-sided, leaking, gone.

Gone. Gone. Gone.

And Clémence too, gone.

Sweet silence.

Philip lies down on the ground, littered with roses, and sleeps under the legs of the horse, like he did before in Autant. Sleeps with the horses in the barn where it is quiet. Safe.

In his dream, Philip sleeps and his hip does not need mending. It was never broken.

Philia smoothes the wet, cool cloth over his forehead. Watches Philip stretch his mouth open and close, open and close, over and over again. A sudden smile plays over his mouth, and then he rests quietly.

She removes the blue rosary from his hip and kisses it, crosses herself, and replaces it carefully on the back of her chair in the corner. Straightening Philip's clothing, smoothing the sheet that covers him, she prays.

Madame Corneille slips her own version of a rosary over the back of Philia's chair and walks quietly back into the kitchen.

Baptiste comes onto the porch and stretches his arms above his head, yawns, and scratches at his neck. He puts his hat on and clumps heavily, one step at a time, down the porch steps. He reaches the bottom step and scans the yard, hands on his hips.

As if he owns the place, sniffs Madame Corneille from behind the door. Such arrogance.

He walks over to the chicken coop. Feet splayed, he pees against the wire fence, scattering the chickens. There is a moment when he feels a crawling sensation pass from groin to hand, as if someone is watching him. He shakes himself three times and shoves his penis into his overalls.

Madame Corneille comes out of the house, down the porch steps, holding a tall, sweating glass of water. She closes her eyes and tips her head back to drink. Her throat is exposed, a blue vein thumps against soft brown skin. Her eyes are closed and the water slides down, trickling out the side of her mouth, down that smooth throat into the bodice of her dress, leaving a small, dark stain.

—Aaaaaaah! she breathes, wiping her mouth. She opens her eyes wide. —Now that's good water. You are staying for supper M Baptiste, she says, nearing the coop. —Would you do the honours of selecting two fine hens for tonight? We need them plucked, of course.

She breathes deeply. Smelling the pee, she pulls at her collar to close it more tightly.

—I will surely do that for her, for Madame Philia, says Baptiste, lighting a cigarette. His eyes don't leave the stain on her bodice.

Madame Corneille brings her hand to the stain, covers her throat. Baptiste looks up.

—I don't need an axe, he drawls. —I like to wring their necks. It's neater that way.

His hands mimic the quick clutching and wrenching. His hands are level with her throat, measuring the width of her throat.

She stares at him and sees something of the Old Evil.

—And I cut their heads off after, he finishes, his hands coming together in front of her with a slap.

—Oh yes, of course, she says, taking a step back. —Yes, I see.

Evelyn can hear them talking. She sees Baptiste's hands come up to the half-breed's neck. Something buzzes nearby. Her own throat constricts and she mangles the edge of her apron. His hands come down and Evelyn lets out her breath.

Baptiste turns towards her. He saunters over to the truck.

—So, you'll kill chickens? she whispers, passing him the jar of ragotte they keep in the truck.

—Apparently so, he slurps a mouthful of the tepid alcohol, rinses his mouth, and spits towards the trees.

—Is that the payment? We kill two chickens and it's paid?

—Seems so.

—Which one did it? The white one or that one?

—The white one.

—Maybe she has a different price then! Maybe you should ask her.

—Doesn't matter to me.

—But what if she asks for money? hisses Evelyn.

—Doesn't matter, we don't have any.

—Yes, but she could ask, she mutters angrily.

—Could ask. Doesn't matter though, does it? He turns away from his wife and looks at the chickens, pecking where his pee dots the ground.

From where they stand together on the porch, Philia and Madame Corneille believe Baptiste Trefflé is smiling. They cross themselves in silence.

▦ Talon 1914

[   ]   A small, slightly stooped man wearing a long butcher's apron in front of a store bearing the sign, "Magasin Poisseau." A tight-lipped woman beside him, staring at the camera with suspicion.

Philia:

I watch the woman make her way down the street. She is tall, thin, and dark-skinned. She wears her hair in a long black braid down the middle of her back. She walks pigeon-toed to better balance burdens. A little one clutches a hand-ful of her skirt from behind. A smaller one in a sack on her back. I watch her.

She steps into the store. Stands still as her eyes become accustomed to the gloom. She is Madame Marie-Ange Corneille.

She walks to the high counter and places her list in front of Mme Poisseau. With jewelled claws, Mme Poisseau swoops to grab the paper and reads out loud: —beenz, fleur, tée, sukr . . . What is this?! I can't read this! Is this lan-guage? What does this say?

The mother's dark eyes flash with rage then, in the same heartbeat, dim and lower, fix on the floorboards. She shuffles back and steps on the child's feet. The child squeaks but makes no complaint. The mother puts her small leather bag on the counter. The clink of coin might help the translation.

Mme Poisseau sighs one of the long-suffering sighs usually reserved for M Poisseau and his small brown jug. She reaches for the pouch.

I reach forward, take the paper, and push the bag back into the woman's hand.

—She needs beans, flour, tea, sugar, as well as material for a dress, tobacco, salt, and matches.

—Oh, Madame Philia, tu t'accotes avec ce type ces jours ci? Mme Poisseau sneers.

—Je m'accote d'avantage avec les truits du village, quand elles ont besoin de l'aide, ma chère. Et la main de ton Paul? Pas trop de douleure, j'espère? N'oubliez pas que j'ai longuant nécessaire pour laver la plaie.

—Non, euh, oui, euh merci, oui, Madame.

—Bon. Je trouve les petites choses que j'ai besoin, tandis que vous aidiez cette femme, ensuite, j'aurais besoin de votre aide, si vous êtes disponible?

Mme Poisseau nods stiffly, without meeting my eyes. Smiles, bec pincé, to the other woman.

I finger the bolt of blue cloth the little girl brings.

—C'est un beau bleu, comme tes yeux, puce.

The mother and the midwife stand. We stand, side by side.

Philia remembers to ask Madame Poisseau for cuttings of her geraniums and buys a black school exercise book. It becomes her work to collect memories for those to come.

[   ]   Marie-Ange Corneille holding a baby in her arms; her husband Gaston stands frowning beside her. *Shut up for five minutes! Christly bawling worse than a calf!*

Philia:
I feel the kicking stop. I glance outside. Shade-wise, it is 5 o'clock. A warm spot glows in the base of my spine. I sigh and finish slicing the bread.

That night I hear sibilant whispers, —Mamie? Mamie?

Delphis places his hand on my hip. —Not long now, einh?

—Tomorrow, I grunt.

He massages my back with his fist. I smile in the dark. A good man, that Delphis. A very good man.

The next day, the déclenchement, a letting go. I am in the garden picking beans and squeezing every spider I can find. If it rains, no one will expect a new mother to be out doing hard work.

—Madame Philia? Madame Philia! Come quick! It's the baby, it's coming! Papa says to hurry!

I smile to the girl, wipe the dirt from my hands onto my long apron.

—J'arrive la petite, j'arrive.

I pick up my bag lying in the shade of the willow, pat the tree, and go to bring the next child of Talon into the world.

Rubis:
Last push, ma belle, come on now good girl good girl big push to get this out now!

—I can't, Rubis. I'm too tired, just pull it out, cut it out I don't care, I just can't anymore!

—Listen now. Listen to me, look at me. Look at me. You've done the hard part already. You just need to do this last little part. Think of washing clothes . . .

—Ah non!

—Yes, yes girl, think of washing clothes and now you have to wring out the clothes, right? Can't have them stay just wet for days and days and days. Now come on, squeeze the clothes girl! That's right, that's right, good girl. Good girl, there there now, yes, yes a little more, there, there. Good. Good girl! All done. Rest now, ma belle. Rest and we will bring you your daughter when she is all cleaned up. Then we'll get you cleaned up too, all right?

I look over to the new mother's sister, France, and smile weakly. All of us are exhausted. It has been a long delivery, but a safe one. Thank you Vièrge Marie. France brings the baby, newly washed and swaddled, to her mother. She gently massages the other woman's breast to stimulate the milk and shows her how to make sure the little mouth is properly latched on.

While the new mother nurses her daughter, I weigh the afterbirth with a steady hand and a careful eye. It is intact, so no need to go back in there and pull anything else out, merci encore la Vièrge. I pull it apart and look through it. It is a strong, healthy colour. This birth will end well, thank God. I cross myself quickly, remembering other recent births that haven't ended so well.

—France? I nod my head toward the afterbirth now wrapped in the bloody sheet her sister was lying on.

France shrugs her shoulders and turns away, cooing to her new niece.

I pass the back of my hand over my forehead. This is the worst part, really. What to do about the cleaning up. No one has an opinion until I make a move. Then all of a sudden, what I take for granted, what is common sense, is wrong. I have learned to be blunt. To be cautious is a waste of time.

—Do you want to feed this to the pigs? Or do you want to burn it? I ask.

I see that the new mother has that glazed look about her, and my heart softens. I remember that I too have a family at home waiting for me.

—Well? How do you want me to do this?

Both women ignore me so I take up the sheet and walk away from the bed, tightly covering the extra of birth.

Outside I find the husband pacing and smoking a pipe that glows from constant use.

—Here, I'll trade you this, I say, giving him the bundle, —for this, and I pluck the pipe. I take a few quick puffs.

—This? he stutters. What is this?

—Bury it far from the house. Better yet, burn it if you can. They are sheets that will never come clean again.

I have to laugh at the look on his face. He is paler than is necessary under the circumstances. I know he is thinking, how can this all be blood? All from his wife?

—She is fine and you have a lovely, strong, healthy daughter. Don't worry, they all bleed like that. Think about that next time you want a tumble in the sheets, einh? I laugh to reassure him.

*I tap the pipe bowl with the heel of my boot before slipping it back into his
mouth.*

*He turns from me, pipe clenched between his teeth, and I know he will bury
the sheets, probably throwing up all the while. He is a young man, just a colt
really. The sight of his face makes me smile. He looks like Marc when Raoul
was born.*

*France comes out from the bedroom when she hears the kettle boiling. I pull
small bundles of herbs from my leather bag and set them down.*

*Without looking up I say, — Here are some things you can use. I point to the
first bundle, —Sage, to make the milk come. Dill for the baby. I point to the
second bundle. —If she gets too much air at first she'll have a lot of gas, this will
help. —And camomile for the rest of you, I say, holding up the third bundle.*

*France nods. —Thank you Rubis, for coming, I couldn't do it on my own, and
her, she rolls her eyes in exasperation.*

*—We are all like that the first time, remember? I say. —The second time around
she'll pop it out and go back to washing clothes without a second thought.*

*—After what you said about wringing out the clothes, I doubt she will ever
wash clothes again! laughs France.*

*—Well then maybe the husband will have to wash the clothes from now on, I
say, closing up my bag.*

—Oh yes. And I am sure he'll start cooking meals too! snorts France.

*—There are miracles everyday, France, I say slowly, — but a man cooking a proper
meal? Christ would make them all walk on water first, I finish in a whisper and
a wink.*

*We both laugh. —Well, you know where I am if you need anything else. I am
going home to watch my own miracle sleep for an hour or so before the sun
puts him on his feet. Good night Madame France.*

—Good night Madame Rubis.

France walks me over the threshold and squeezes my arm before I step out into
the darkness. —Be careful riding home Rubis Morin, she says softly.

I raise my hand, wide open behind me, to show that I have heard. I am just too
tired to talk anymore.

My lovely horse is sleeping at the fence, still wearing the blanket I pulled over
him when I first arrived. Quietly, I make soothing hello noises. The horse
whinnies sleepily. His velvet nose butting my shoulder, he nods as if to say,
—Yes, this is you and this is me standing here in the cold, again. Let's go.

I rub his forehead lovingly, soothing the long lines of muscle down his neck
and sides. I mount and we are off down the road, stars twinkling overhead. I
imagine what we look like, rider and mount, one graceful liquid shadow,
almost invisible, I hope.

[   ]   Inside a barn. Léo plays the fiddle. Philia, Evelyn Trefflé, and a
young Clémence are seated to the left of him on high-backed chairs. A very
muscular, tall man seated to the right of Léo on a bale of hay. This is
Baptiste Trefflé.

> *At least we can play music.*
> *She knows more than she is saying.*
> *I feel safer knowing someone can help with the delivery.*
> *I want to remember it, just like this.*
> *Say one word, bitch, and I'll kill you where you sit.*

Philia:
It's a fall party
most families from Talon are here,
even that new family, Trefflé.
Mamans, young wives, brothers, snotty nosed kids,
clothes too big, too small,
or none at all just a piquée and des bas de laine.

I have come to play the mouth-organ.

My husband pulls me from my brothers
a gleam in his eye
to a corner
where a young boy holds his crooked arm
close to his belly, like an old man, bent
a piece of piecrust clutched
in his other fist.

I push up my dress sleeves.
Delphis gently holds the boy in his lap
and pulls out his watch
for the child's attention, for the smooth tug that
must follow till swollen muscles allow
the graceful
slip of bone on bone,
in place.

The child opens his mouth to cry
but the pain is over and his eyes follow
this lady.
He traces with his fingers the bulging veins
in my forearms.

I blow his nose
I blow my nose
and pull out the mouth-organ to play.

En roulant ma boule roulant
En roulant ma boule,
Derrière chez nous, ya t-un étang,
En roulant ma boule,
Trois beaux canards s'en vont baignant,
Rouli, roulant, ma boule roulant,
En roulant ma boule roulant,

En roulant ma boule.

Trois beaux canards s'en vont baignant,
Le fils du roi s'en va chassant.

Le fils du roi s'en va chassant,
Avec son grand fusils d'argent.

Avec son grand fusils d'argent,
Visa le noir, tua le blanc.

Visa le noir, tua le blanc,
O fils du roi, tu es méchant!

Talon 1931

Clémence retches violently into the pig-slop bucket. Her hair dangles in sweaty, greasy strings. Evelyn looks up from where she lies on the bed dandling Urbain.

—Clémence, be careful there! You're throwing up on the floor! What is wrong with you girl? This is the third morning you wake me with the sound of your vomit.

Clémence raises her face to her mother. Evelyn notices the dark-blue circles under her eyes, the sallow complexion, and dryness around the mouth. Clémence is trembling lightly and covered in a film of sweat. Her dress sticks to her back and under the arms.

—I don't know, Maman, she croaks. —I feel sick, I . . . and she is wracked by another spasm.

—Well, get some food in to your belly. Sometimes in the morning I'd feel like that and a piece of bread . . . Evelyn stops herself and looks more closely at her daughter. Sick? In the morning? No, impossible, she never leaves the farm, never leaves my sight, always with Reuville or Roland or Bapt– . . . no. She puts it from her mind.

She says, —Clémence, make some tea, your father will be in. And he will want some breakfast before leaving for town. There's some fish left over from last night and oh! Quick! Bring a fresh cloth for Urbain, he is a real shitter this morning. Aren't you, mon Urbain? Yes you are, she croons into the baby's soft belly. —Pew! Clémence, the cloth! Hurry up!

Clémence struggles to her feet. She pushes the slop bucket back under the sink and stumbles from the room to outside, where the fresh cloths dry on the line.

Once outside, the fresh air revives her. She fixes on the white squares flapping in the breeze and walks slowly towards them.

I wish those diapers were sails, she thinks. Sails on a ship that could take me far from here. I can't stay here one more day. If he touches me again, I'll surely kill myself. It is not right for him to do that. It hurts too much and I tell him to stop but . . . she yanks the cloths angrily from the line. "Maman is too sick with Urbain," what is he talking about? She doesn't look sick to me.

She pulls the last of the diapers from the line, goes into the house, and throws them at her mother still in the bed.

—Clémence! Clémence come back here, I need you to change the baby. Clémence! shrills Evelyn.

Clémence is already upstairs, kneeling by the small bed, the one place in all the world that she feels safe. He never bothers me here, she thinks feverishly, not with the boys sleeping so close.

She pulls the small bundle from underneath the bed. It is an old ragbag, mended to hold all her possessions. She touches each item reverently: socks, a toque, her good skirt, and two shirts, the comb she received from the passing peddler who took a fancy to her red hair the day he rode through Autant, selling needles, cloth, and whatnots for the kitchen. She fervently kisses the rosary her godmother gave her for good luck and the small prayer card of la Vièrge Marie.

Satisfied that everything is in order, she closes up the bag, stuffing it quickly back under the bed. From under the quilt she pulls the only warm thing she posesses. It is an oversized black-and-red plaid woolen coat rescued from the lumber camp she had stumbled upon. She was planning to cut it down for 'Ti Paul, a surprise for him at Christmas. But he won't need it now. It becomes a gift for herself.

—Clémence Eugéenie Trefflé! shrieks Evelyn. —Get down here this instant! You may not listen to me, but when your father gets in, you will have to listen to him! You will answer to him, ma belle Clémence! When I tell him how disobedient you are, we'll see how fast you run then. Are you listening to me?

Clémence sighs and folds the coat back under her quilt. Gingerly, she stands again, hands automatically going to the small of her back and her stomach. She heads down the stairs into the full fury of her mother and the squalling Urbain.

Baptiste is in the shed, drinking from the bottle of whiskey he has stashed under the seat of the truck. He will take Clémence into town, buy her something. Buy her a dress or a dolly or something. On the way back, he will stop a ways past the graveyard, and . . . he fingers the horsehair blanket stashed under the seat.

He hears Roland bawling out Reuville about something. They are coming closer; he hastily pushes the blanket and the bottle back under the seat, and slams the door.

—What the hell is all the racket about? he bellows.

—Roland says I can't come with you. He says it's his turn but it's not, it's my turn! screams Reuville.

Roland cuffs his brother hard across the head.

—Shut up dummy! I am going because I am the oldest and Papa needs help with the heavy equipment. You said I could go this time, remember Papa? Roland finishes, standing tall in front of his father, trying to keep the pleading out of voice.

Baptiste scratches his chin. His hand thumps heavily on Roland's shoulder. As he speaks, his fingers dig into the soft muscle.

—No, you are to stay here and put up the rest of that fence.

—But Papa! explodes Roland, wincing.

—Ha! cackles Reuville.

—And you, continues Baptiste, digging the fingers of his other hand into Reuville's shoulder, —will help him.

—But Papa!

—No arguments. Clémence is coming to town with me.

Both boys look at him, their jaws dropping.

—Clémence? they echo in disbelief, the pain in their shoulders forgotten for the moment.

—Yes, Clémence, Baptistes breathes, relaxing his grip on them.

—But Papa, begins Roland.

Baptiste tightens his fingers around the big nerve near the collarbone and Roland bends at the knees, hissing.

—I said Clémence, and I mean Clémence. No one else. Now get to that fence.

Roland looks his father hard in the face, but says nothing. He wrenches his shoulder from Baptiste's grip, turns on his heel, and strides angrily towards the door.

—Hey! barks Baptiste, reaching behind him for the hammer, —You forgot this! He throws it to the ground in front of Roland.

Stiffly, warily, his eyes never leaving Baptiste's boots, Roland stoops.

Baptiste takes a half-empty bucket of nails from the shelf and unceremoniously dumps its contents in front of Reuville.

—Pick those up, he says, a twisted grin on his face, —you'll need them for the fence.

Reuville scowls as he bends forward.

Baptiste kicks his son viciously in the backside, sending him sprawling on the hard-packed floor, face first into the nails.

—That's for causing trouble with your brother. Now get out of my sight! I don't want to see either of you until I get back from town.

He turns back to the truck and yanks open the hood.

Reuville's eyes begin to water in pain and indignation, but he quickly scoops the nails into the bucket. Clutching his bottom, he runs backwards out of the garage after his brother.

—I hate him! he sniffles, as they leave the yard.

Roland snorts, —It's okay, he hates you too.

Reuville lightly punches him on the arm. —I hate you, he says gruffly.

—Yah? Well I hate you too, says Roland, punching him back.

Reuville smiles to himself. —You know who I really hate? he says, —Clémence. "Clémence, that bitch," he growls deeply, imitating his father. —I hate Clémence for being able to go with him, he sighs. —She always gets to go with him. Remember, he used to take all of us? Now it's just Clémence, Clémence, Clémence . . . ever since Urbain was born, Clémence, Clémence, Clémence!

Roland is hardly listening to his little brother's rant. Anger boils up inside his heart; he has had enough of these bullshit beatings from the old man. He stops and turns, intending to go back to the shed.

He breathes deeply, straightens the sleeves of his threadbare jacket and reaches towards Reuville to tell him to go on without him.

The sudden movement jars his shoulder. Pain deflates his anger, quick as that. He stifles the urge to cry and continues walking, head down and scowling.

—If he wants smelly old Clémence, he can have her, he says. —She hates going with the old man, and I think if he stays mean today, I'm glad it's not me going. At least she can get kicked for a while instead of us, einh? he grins crookedly at his brother.

69

—Yah, says Reuville, then he sobers, —Is that why Philip left do you think? Tired of getting kicked in the backside? Do you think Papa kicks Clémence in the bum, Roland?

Roland ignores the question.

—Probably kicks what ever he lands his shitty boots on. Of course he kicks her in the bum! Probably the twat too, he snickers maliciously, delighting in his foul mouth.

Reuville laughs, not sure what a twat is, but figuring that it must be another word for legs. That's why Clémence walks so slowly these days, he thinks, the old man's been kicking her in the legs. This thought cheers him up.

He looks up at his big brother. —Race 'ya! he screams, taking off, the nail bucket jangling dangerously in his hand.

From the kitchen window Clémence watches her brothers disappear from the yard. She sees her father striding toward the house, smoothing his long hair back. She braces herself, realizing that she is to go once more with him into town. She envisions her bundle upstairs. This will be the last time.

She hastily sets the table for him, not forgetting the bowl for his cigarette ashes, then limps upstairs to fetch her things. Her mind is racing ahead, figuring how she will get the coat and everything hidden so he won't suspect anything.

While he eats, she tries to slip out the door unnoticed.

—Hey girl! he drawls, what's the lump? What are you carrying there?

—It's a pillow, for my bum, the truck seats are hard, she mutters, head down.

For some reason, Baptiste finds this uproariously funny. He nearly chokes on his coffee, cigarette dangling and jerking over the edge of the table.

Before he can recover, Clémence slips through the door and walks as quickly as she can towards the shed.

—Baptiste? calls Evelyn, coming from the bedroom. —What's so funny? she asks. —Where's Clémence? I have some chores for her to do today. That girl is always disappearing . . .

Baptiste coughs thickly and spits into the bowl for his ashes. He tips his chair back and looks at his wife, holding Urbain.

—If you don't let that damned kid walk, his legs are just going to fall off, he says, disgust colouring his words.

—Oh, the floor is too cold just now, and he's not too heavy, really, she says, shifting her burden to her other hip.

Urbain shoves a fist into his mouth. Evelyn gives him a piece of bread from Baptiste's plate. Baptiste stubs his smoke into the remaining pile of toast.

—Going into town today, he grunts.

—Roland told me this morning. He wants to look at those rifles again and I told him . . .

—Roland isn't coming. Clémence is, he says lighting another cigarette.

Evelyn looks at him.

—I need Clémence here today, there's all the washing to do and the floors need . . .

—She's coming with me, he says.

—But she has to . . .

—Do it yourself, he snaps. Get off your fat ass and do the work yourself. Jésus! My first wife wasn't half so big as you and she did twice the work.

—Baptiste! she is shocked by his rebuke. —You know I do what I can; what with all the complications of Urbain's birth, and since 'Ti Paul died, I have just been so sad. I just don't have the strength to do everything I used to. My back hurts all the time and my legs pain me so. You've seen the veins, she says plaintively.

—Yah, well your damned veins are about all I've seen. We'll be back at supper, he says gruffly, getting up from the table.

The chair tips back and falls over. He doesn't pick it up.

—Try not to be too sad, he sneers, turning away from her accusing stare.

—Baptiste . . . Baptiste! Evelyn calls, but she is talking to the air.

He is already gone, shrugging into his jacket and pulling on his hat as the door slams behind him.

—What's gotten into him today? she muses aloud to the baby. —Einh? What's the matter with the Papa today? Maybe he's sad today too. When he drinks, he gets this way. Don't think about it bébé, she croons softly into Urbain's hair. —Don't think about it.

Ignoring the ugly feelings deep inside her, Evelyn begins to move the plates and bowls on the table, back and forth. She hums, "En roulant ma boule roulant, en roulant ma boule, trois beaux canards s'en vont baignant, le fils du roi s'en va chassant . . ."

The song sounds mournful and Urbain begins to fret. She absently strokes his arm and continues her humming, continues to move the plates, back and forth, back and forth, and sees nothing.

—Good thing you brought that pillow, einh? laughs Baptiste. Clémence slumps against the door, her head bumping against the window at every rut. She closes her eyes. A shudder runs through her body.

—What did you want from town then? I said I'd buy you a doll or something, einh? First I'll have a beer with the boys and then to Poisseau's store, he continues as if she is in any way connected to the conversation.

—What about 'Ti Paul? she murmurs through half-closed lips.

—What's that? he says, reaching for the bottle under the seat.

—You said we were going to visit 'Ti Paul's grave, she says flatly, still not opening her eyes. —Back there, you promised.

—What? Oh yeah, right, the grave. Well, you go ahead while I'm in the bar. Not like he's going to know if we were there or not, he mutters. —Go see him! Pray for the lucky little bastard, dead before the bad stuff happens to him, he finishes, swallowing deeply.

Clémence opens her eyes and looks straight ahead, an idea forming in her mind. —I'll go to the cemetery then walk back home. I don't need a new doll.

—Walk home? he looks at her sharply, —Are you crazy? You wait for me beside the truck when you're finished your little visit. Wait for me, like always. Do you hear me Clémence?

She says nothing, turns her head towards the window, so he won't see the smile creeping into her eyes. 'Ti Paul, you saved me today, she thinks.

—Do you hear me? he repeats, swerving to hit a pothole.

Her head jerks up and he catches her under the chin with the butt of the bottle.

—Yes, I hear you, she mumbles, still not looking at him, feeling the cold glass at her throat.

—Good, he says, drunkenly satisfied that she will obey him. —Good girl.

He brings the bottle to his mouth and drinks.

Clémence buries her face in the jacket bundle she holds in her lap and softly rocks herself to ease the pain between her legs. She hums quietly, so quietly that Baptiste does not hear, "En roulant ma boule en roulant, en roulant ma boule, visa le noir, tua le blanc . . ."

—I am going now, she calls out to the empty graveyard. —Paulo? Can you hear me? C'est Clémence.

She calls in the voice she used to calm Paul with when he was angry. —I am going to live with Madame Philia because, well, because, it is time for me to go. Like it was time for you to go, remember? 'Ti Paul's grave is not the smallest, and it is not the best tended, but Clémence does what she can every time she visits, pulling weeds here, placing a handful of wild flowers in the crook of the wooden cross. Today, she recolours the name with a stub of grease pencil:

Paul Trefflé
Avec les Anges

She looks around furtively, terrified that her father will appear and take her away again.

Saying a quick "Je Vous Salut Marie," she touches the cross one more time. Then she touches her heart with two fingers. It's how they say hello and goodbye to each other in this village. The men touch the brim of their caps with two fingers. But Clémence isn't a man, she doesn't wear a hat, and she isn't acknowledging 'Ti Paul with her head. She wraps him for her heart.

Turning, she walks resolutely towards the village and she seeks shelter under the porch steps of the bank. It is directly in front of the bar. From here she can keep an eye on her father's truck.

Clémence stays well hidden, her huge jacket keeping her warm and dry. She will wait until her father leaves town before going to Massie's. She cannot risk him finding her on the open road.

She carefully combs her hair, braiding it neatly and fixing it with a piece of rawhide. As best she can, scooping water carefully from the puddles under the steps, she wipes the tears and snot from her face. She changes into her clean skirt, noticing how tight the waist band has become, and throws her underwear as far into the darkness as she can. She awkwardly tucks in her shirt and takes her rosary from the ragbag.

Kneeling on her old coat, she threads the beads with a practiced ease. If she is able to go through the prayers one hundred times without stopping, her most fervent desire will come true. She waits and she prays, like she was taught.

Baptiste staggers from the bar in the five o'clock darkness. He urinates on the front tire of the truck, opens the driver's side door, and peers drunkenly into the dark interior. She can hear him curse. He bangs the hood heavily and stumbles to the back of the truck, moving things around, yanking the tarp up, cursing the heavier objects. The search seems to exhaust him. Clémence sees him slump against the truck and pull his hands through his hair. He does not say her name. She is suddenly afraid of the power he will have over her if he says her name.

No, the last thing she will see and hear of him is his evil. She blocks her ears, the rosary dangling under her chin, and closes her eyes. Fervently she continues to pray, the beads slipping silently through her fingers. She rocks on her haunches and prays.

Baptiste slaps his hat back onto his head, lights a cigarette, and looks up and down the street. He makes to cross the street, towards the post office. Gaston Corneille comes out from behind the bar and says something to Baptiste. They both laugh loudly and Gaston wobbles over to Baptiste and slaps him on the back. Gaston says something else as he stands near the truck tire and urinates. Baptiste shakes his head and laughs again. Gaston zips himself up and helps Baptiste into the cab of the truck before continuing across the street. He turns and gives the two-finger wave as Baptiste rumbles past him.

Gaston stops in front of the bank, rocks back forth on his heels, lights a smoke, then walks on, humming, "En roulant ma boule en roulant, en roulant ma boule, visa le noir, tua le blanc, o! fils du roi tu es méchant!"

Clémence knows someone is there, in front of her, but she does not open her eyes, she does not stop praying. She is nearly finished and when she opens her eyes everything will be all right. It has to be.

. . . Sainte Marie, Mère de Dieu, priez pour nous pécheurs, maintenant et à l'heure de notre mort. Amen.

One hundred.
There.
Ready or not, here I come.

Gaston Corneille sits on the churchyard fence smoking a cigarette. He watches Clémence disappear into the back of a stranger's truck, heading out of town down Massie's way. Two dogs, one blonde, one black, race out from behind the post office. They tail the truck as far as the graveyard, barking their goodbyes until they are hoarse.

Gaston sings in a loud clear voice,

> Un Canadien errant,
> Bani de ses foyers,
> Un Canadien errant,
> Bani de ses foyers,
> Parcourait en pleurant
> Des pays étrangers
> Parcourait en pleurant
> Des pays étrangers.

He touches two fingers to his cap.

Baptiste goes there when he stops fire. It begins with a low, slow rumble. The thunder behind his eyes gathering, rolling, roiling, obliterating light and sound until only Itself can be heard. He goes there and does God's work, returning to this place when God is finished with him, finished pouring the power through him.

He thumbs the ribbons in his black book. In this book are the necessary prayers and specific Bible verses for healing, written in delicate blue ink in his mother's hand. Baptiste looks in disdain at his father's first family tree:

Oréuss Trefflé – 1800 + Marie Pique

|

Télèsphore Trefflé – 1839/1874 + Zoë Chamberland
Bruno Trefflé – 1840/1874 + Oralie Bisson
Antoine Trefflé – 1841/ + Pulchérie Coeur

Régina Trefflé – 1842 décédée bébé
Rélina Trefflé – 1843 décédée bébé
Alphonse Trefflé – 1845 décédé bébé
Marie Pique décédée 1846

Pauvre Marie Pique, pathetic, he grunts and grins to himself. Now, he scans the page for his line, his wise Maman Giselle's promises. She had written down the succession of children he would have, before they were born, before he was even married. She had told him he would take two wives and have seven children. He had dutifully filled in the dates and the children's names as they arrived. Now he had only to wait for the last girl, the one he would give his mother's book to.

Oréuss Trefflé + Giselle Pique (deuxième femme)

Baptiste Trefflé 1868 + Evelyn Casavant

garçon et fille – 1916- PHILIP + LOUISE
garçon – 1917 ROLAND
fille – 1918 CLÉMENCE
garçon –1919 REUVILLE
garçon – 1919 décédé bébé PAUL
garçon – 1920 URBAIN
fille – 1921

He smiles to himself, a satisfied smile. Marie Pique had only bore one son to the old man, that was all she needed. Baptiste was the seventh child and Giselle gave everything she knew to him, only to him. Les dons came to him, it was his birthright, his gift for surviving; he was a gift, as would be the last girl child promised, the seventh born from the seventh born.

'Ti Paul died to make way for the girl. This Clémence girl is of no use to him except to serve and be of comfort. It is the principle of the matter, the sense of having been cheated out of what is rightfully his to own and do with as he pleases that drives him to his book, to this chair on this day.

She must pay for disobeying, for having run away from her responsibilities, he thinks grimly. She will not disobey me again.

Baptiste strokes the silk ribbon, red silk to stop fire, and listens for the thunder. He knows it will come, it always does. He wills the thunder. He closes his eyes and commands it to appear, to do his bidding, now. Find Clémence.

Evelyn watches him warily from the kitchen. Why isn't he out looking for Clémence? She can't understand why he is just sitting there with his book of prayers, stock-still in the chair facing east. The book comes out only when someone needs to be helped, but no one has come here today have they? The villagers all go to that Massie woman. Patrique and Léo Morin, they too are healers around here; no one comes to Baptiste Casavant, yet. He has a way of making people come to him for help, part of his gift, his charm, Evelyn supposes.

She steals anxious glimpses towards her husband as she busies herself in the kitchen, ready to keep the children away from him. There is little danger of that though, they are all well trained enough to know not to bother Papa when he has the book out. Even Urbain is unusually quiet in his highchair, watching.

Baptiste's eyes are closed as he rocks gently back and forth, riding the thunder to where Clémence is.

—No one is up this early Clémence, except the wicked and weary, smiles Philia, shuffling into the kitchen. —Are those biscuits I smell?

Clémence looks up at her, not moving her head, just lifting her eyes and looking up through her hair. She hasn't braided it yet and it looks stringy and dirty.

—Ma foie du bon Dieu enfant! No need to look at me so wild. I just want to talk to you Clémence.

Philia stands behind Clémence and embraces her. She pulls her hair back from her face and runs her fingers through the tangled mess, humming distractedly.

—I am sorry Madame Philia. I don't know what is wrong with me. I was feeling sick and a little hungry so I thought I would get up and make some biscuits for breakfast. I am sorry if I woke you Madame. You know, I thought it would be better here, but I have been here two days and I still feel awful. I am tired of feeling tired and awful.

Philia's hand caresses the girl's forehead, pausing to take Clémence's temperature with the back of her hand.

—Do you want to feel better Clémence? Not so tired and sick to your stomach all the time? she sighs a long, heavy sigh.

—Yes, Madame, I really do, chokes Clémence through the tears that threaten her voice. —I must be crazy! One minute I am angry, then I am so sad I want to die, then I am happier than I ever thought possible. I am happy to be here, but please Madame, can you help me? Can you make me not crazy anymore?

Philia finishes braiding her hair and pats her on the shoulder. She walks briskly towards the stove.

—We'll have your lovely biscuits and I'll make you some tea. Then you'll sleep and when you wake up you'll feel better. I promise.

Clémence lays her head on her arms. Her breath makes a cloudy mist on the table's surface. She traces the figure eight over and over again on the table. She closes her eyes.

Philia comes back with a cup of tea and sets it down before the girl.

—It is crocus tea, tea that will help you feel better. It is quite awful though, she laughs, watching the girl screw up her face at the first sip. She moves the honey jar towards Clémence.

Clémence hesitates then plucks a spoon from the jar and scoops up a great dollop.

—What is wrong with me? she asks, in a small voice.

Philia looks intently at the girl. She speaks slowly, her eyes never leaving Clémence's face.

—Sometimes a woman's body needs help to clean itself, she says softly.

Sometimes we become blocked. This tea will help you not be blocked any-more. This tea will help you bleed and you will clean yourself, Clémence. You need to bleed.

Clémence starts and her tea sloshes onto the table.

—Bleed? she yelps, —I don't want to bleed! I haven't had my time for, for months now. I don't ever want to get them again. Not here, not now . . .

She pushes her chair back from the table and rises shakily.

—Clémence, Philia puts her hand on the girl's arm.

—Clémence, she says again, her other hand coming up to cup the girl's cheek. —You will bleed because you need to clean out whatever is making you sick. You understand that, don't you? When you are sick and you throw up, that is helping you to clean out your system. When you cut yourself, you always let the wound bleed a little, to clean it, right? Yes?

—But I don't want to bleed. It hurts when I bleed, Clémence whimpers. —It hurts when it bleeds there.

—It will hurt a little, Clémence, but it gets better with time. I promise you Clémence, it will get better. You are safe here, little one. Safe to get better, and we will take care of you. You know that don't you? Yes.

Clémence watches a tear fall into her teacup.

Philia speeds up her little pep talk. —You were so good with that little Casavant boy, and he hurt like crazy. Then he felt better didn't he? We won't let you bleed until you die Clémence, just long enough to clean you out. There will be la jeune Marie who can help you, of course, and Monsieur Patrique and Monsieur Léo, my brothers. We will do this and we will help you Clémence. There is a time to feel sick and a time to feel bet-ter. You want to feel better. Drink the tea Clémence.

—I am afraid, she mumbles, watching another teardrop hit the tea.

—Yes, yes, of course you are chouette. She hands the girl a handkerchief. Clémence blows her nose.

—How about some biscuits to go with that tea? Are you feeling well enough for biscuits? I am hungry too, come to think of it. Those biscuits sure smell good to me now! And we should eat them before the kid wake up, you know what a little pig that Léonie can be when it comes to biscuits and honey . . .

Baptiste smiles through the thunder. This is fine after all. That woman knows what she is doing. It is the oldest power isn't it? This cleaning of the house with blood.

He relaxes in his chair, knowing that after Clémence begins to bleed she will feel nothing but pain, and that will keep her quiet for at least three days. And on the third day, yes, the third day, he will go after her and bring her home.

[   ]   Philia and Evelyn stand to one side in front of a grotto, neither is smiling. Clémence stands on the other side placing flowers at the foot of the statue of Marie. Two women and a girl. On the back of the photo is inscribed: "La Fête des Reines, 1931." *You can't really have my daughter. I have pledged her to Our Lord's mother. Marie will be her protection now. No one can hurt her now.*

[   ]   A priest in a long, black cassock, shaking the hand of the very tall, very muscular Baptiste Trefflé. Baptiste looks into the camera. The priest is looking sideways at Baptiste. *If you need anything, see l'Abbé Morin when he passes through again. He can get you almost anything you need. What he won't give you, come and see me!*

This power
fierce and forever
shaping portals from flower and stone alike.

To be latched on the back of the big sky

braided with thunder
it will be ridden—

as the space between pictures
ridden—
as the velvet moss to stone to
break it.

x Rubis

Talon 1962

The priest is busy at the altar, fiddling with the chalice and the cloths. The altar boys snigger quietly and nudge each other knowingly when they see him barely touch the water flask to the wine. The priest throws them a dirty look and they swallow their giggles, suddenly intent on the threadbare red carpet at their feet. As they kneel and ring the small bells signalling the bowing of heads during the blessing of the body and the blood, they anticipate the taste of the heady leftover wine.

The priest is still a stranger in this parish, resident for less than twenty years. The church has been here since the early 1900s. The families of Morin, Massie, Corneille, Casavant, Poisseau, Pierpont, and Trefflé have been here longer. They know God lives in this building. They built it; they put Him here.

They know too that there is power outside, in the land and the trees and the water. Walls built by any man cannot contain it. It has no blood, no body. Even walls of flesh will not contain it. There are rituals some know to seek its guidance, to assuage its fury, prayers more powerful than the priest and older than the Church.

Talon 1912

The air is heavy with pollen. Red willow blooms alongside the swollen creek that runs just behind Philia. They claimed this land, their oasis, in the middle of scrub brush and prairie grass. From where she sits, she can smell the towering spruce trees that seem to anchor the land she and Delphis have marked off as their own. She smells grass, dry grass and wet sod drying on the roof of the new house. She hears the lazy sound of bees. Stretching away from her to the left and to the right are the ropes Patrique and Léo rigged up to measure off their own claims. The men are working on the small house they will all share until two more houses can be built. She hears from far off the ring of axe against tree, voices, shouts, and grunts of her husband and brothers.

Philia reads from the small ruby-red book that her father gave her the day she left Montana. She is fully aware of the importance of the gift, the enormity of the love and trust her father has for her to give her his most prized possession. It is in almost perfect condition, as though Rubis had only just finished writing the last entry. Raoul has guarded it with a diligence that speaks of his fierce love for a mother who drowned, mysteriously, shortly after he had left Gaspé to journey to Montana. The pain and confusion surrounding Rubis's death had never left Raoul's heart, and his steadfast devotion to the book was his way of keeping his mother alive, perhaps hoping to one day understand what exactly had happened that night.

One of the first things I did when I arrived was plant the geraniums my mother had given me into pots. They flowered within the first two weeks. Given all the fish fertilizer Marc heaped upon them, it is a wonder they didn't spawn and swim away! Geraniums remind us that good things will come.

x Rubis

—Philia? Philia! Come here woman! bellows Delphis good-naturedly. —And bring the jug for your thirsty old man!

Philia steps from the wagon, button boots ankle deep in the mud of May promise. Geraniums, she thinks. Now where will I get geraniums?

She uses the surveyor's plan, sketched on the back of the Dominion's Land

Act, as a bookmark and tucks Rubis's book into her bedroll. Hunching under the wagon, she heaves out the jug of fresh water.

She breathes deeply of this fresh, clean air. Already she has done what she can to wash out their soiled clothing, hanging it all carefully on the makeshift drying rack Delphis rigged up for her last night. The pots and dishes are neatly stacked underneath the wagon, waiting for her hand to turn the flour and water and spare potatoes into their evening meal.

Her husband leans easily on his long-handled axe, whistling tunelessly, taking in all this place that is theirs. She smiles knowing that he has already made plans and dreams of the crops that will grow from this rich prairie earth.

—Hey you, she says softly, coming up behind him.

She hands him the jug. He uncorks it and tips it up over his shoulder like a whiskey jug. Grinning wickedly, he wipes his mouth with his sleeve. He takes her hand, winter-white, into his own and kisses it.

—Well, what do you think of your old man now, einh? he grins. —Quite the palace, wouldn't you say?

She laughs out loud at his playfullness. The house is dug deep into the ground, about four feet. The roof is flat sod laid over a brace of small logs. It is a crude structure but better than sleeping under the wagon with her brothers snoring and throwing their arms every which way.

—It's absolutely beautiful, she answers with her heart. —Is there enough room inside for all of us? she asks, eyeing the dark interior.

—I guess we'll have to make sure of that. Your brothers are off hunting us a supper to celebrate so we should, ah, maybe we could . . . I told them to take their time . . . he trails off, a faint blush creeping up into his face.

—Why Monsieur Delphis! We are an old married couple and here you are being all shy, she purrs lovingly, slipping her arm through his.

In a heartbeat he lifts her up, letting his axe fall to the ground. Without breaking stride, he turns and ducks his head to enter the house.

A small stand of birch rustles in the breeze. The last thing she sees before she allows his happiness to sweep her into the house are the spruce trees pointing mutely to the horizon.

Together, they begin to dance to a song so old it begins with the smell of stones, and so familiar you don't hear it right away.

[   ]   Philia leans against the wall. Delphis, Patrique, and Léo stand on the roof four feet above the ground, holding out their small glasses to the camera. *I knew these glasses wouldn't break! It's a sign that saint preserves us. If only I can get used to having an underground house, well, it is better than sleeping under the wagon. These flies will be the death of me!*

[   ]   Delphis leans away from the plough harness, as much to keep it straight as to keep himself from falling down. *Take the bloody picture already!*

[   ]   Léo, Patrique, and Delphis stand beside a wagon and a team of horses. *If I don't kill him before the end of the year, I'll have to kill myself.*

Philia has wealth when she reads Rubis's little red book. She reads it as much for the food as for the company. There aren't many white women here yet, although news of a railroad coming through brings more and more men every day. Surely the women will come and then this place will feel more like home, she thinks.

Ever since I can remember there are pigs around. We always butcher in the fall, and then we have a slew of meat to can and to salt. Use all the pig, every bit is good. Which is more than I can say for some people I know.

x Rubis

> **Tongue** *(Not pig though, too small. Same for chickens, too small. It needs to be bigger than your hand.)*
>
> *Cover with cold water, add 1½ tsp. salt to each quart of water; bring to a*

boil. Simmer slowly until tender, about 2 or 3 hours. Keep tongue in the liquid until cool enough to handle, then remove outer skin. Serve hot slices with horseradish.

If your tongue's been smoked or pickled, cover with cold water, bring to a boil, reduce heat, and simmer 3 hours. Keep tongue in the liquid until cool enough to handle then remove outer skin. Serve cold in thin slices.

Heart *(Same rule as tongue, the bigger the better.)*

3-4 lbs. of heart, bacon, 1 cup bread crumbs, onion, salt, pepper, flour, lard

Wash hearts and remove enough of centre part to add the stuffing. Dice bacon and fry until crisp. Combine with breadcrumbs. Season with onion. Fill holes in the heart with stuffing, fasten with skewers. Roll in flour and brown in hot lard. Add a small amount of water. Cover and cook with medium heat until the hearts are done, maybe 2 hours. Thicken the liquid for gravy.

Try with creamed onions and green beans.

Brains

Any quantity of brains can be used. Use sweetbreads if you have no brains. Some men do this all the time.

4 eggs, ½ tsp. salt, ¼ cup milk, 4 tsp. fat, 1 cup precooked brains.

Precook brains by simmering a bit in salted water. Add to this 1 tsp. salt and 1 tbsp. vinegar for every quart of water you use. Drain and drop in cold water.

Beat egg whites until stiff but not dry. Beat yolks with seasoning and liquid. Fold yolk mixture into whites. Fold in chopped brains. Pour into hot greased fry pan and smooth over. Cook slowly until well risen and slightly brown on the bottom; put pan in moderately hot oven for a few minutes to dry out the mixture.

She has met one other couple from down the road, a Monsieur Gaston and Madame Marie-Ange Corneille, a half-breed couple. Gaston seems decent and is invaluable to Delphis when it comes to hunting and trapping in these parts. Madame hasn't said much yet. She is very shy and always very occupied with her own family.

[ ]   Four men standing, smiling. Their rifles rest on the carcass of a bull moose lying prostrate before them. *This is not such a bad place. There is enough game to break a man's heart, if the land doesn't break him first. The air is ripe and sweet with white birch and red willow. Always there are black flies, yes, that's true, but there is a sense of the wild here. There is the possibility of anything.*

Delphis Massie, Patrique and Léo Morin, and their neighbour Gaston Corneille step out of the house into the weak autumn sunshine. The wind is not so strong today; it's a little warmer even. At least it has stopped raining. They stand together then, on some unspoken signal, begin walking. They feel the wet pull of the earth on their boots. Stumps stutter the landscape.

They go through the rituals taught to them by their fathers. A sprinkle of l'eau de Pâques on the doorframes of the new houses to protect against the evil of disease and discord. A sliver of rameau into the cracks of corner fence posts to protect against fire and devastation. The words, half-prayer half-command, used to bless and to repel.

Walking home from the back section they see a coyote running like hell. He comes like a big dog, grinning, tongue lolling.

In one sure movement, Gaston cocks his rifle, sights the coyote, and pulls the trigger. The gunshot splits the air cleanly between hunter and hunted. A flock of sparrows explodes from the trees into the pearl-grey dawn.

The coyote drops not three feet from them. There is the copper smell of spilled blood and the heat of a life leaving its body. It hovers between the four men and the coyote. Gaston spits on the ground.

—Big bastard, einh? he grunts appreciatively.

—Yep, big bastard, agrees Delphis.

—Not scared of us at all, muses Léo, scratching his chin.

—Nope, not scared at all. Think he's got the rabies? says Patrique, taking his knife from the sheath tied to his belt.

—Non, just another stupid coyote. Lots of them 'round here I suppose, says Delphis, searching the flat land for this one's friends and relations. —They always hunt in a pack.

—Hope they aren't all big like this bastard, breathes Delphis.

Patrique kneels down beside the animal and he flips it over onto its back, exposing the genitals. —This was a big bastard all right, he says tenderly. —Should take him home, skin him I guess.

—Non, leave him here. Message for the other big bastards out there. Don't want more of them coming round, einh? Just leave him. They'll get the message, grins Gaston.

Patrique skilfully cuts the sweetbreads from the coyote. —Seems a waste of meat to just leave him here. He stands up, dangling the sac from his hand. —I'll take these for Philia, maybe she can use them for earrings, he laughs.

Gaston doubles over laughing and hooting. He lifts his throat to the sky and howls. Léo, Patrique, and Delphis stand together. Delphis slaps his brothers heartily on the back. The brothers laugh together, joining Gaston with their own howls.

From a small stand of birch, where they haven't cleared yet, comes the anguished howl of a coyote.

The men are quiet. That howl draws another line between hunter and hunted.

The four men, suddenly sobered, continue walking home. Their boot outlines, the heels, pool with water.

They make tracks a child could follow. The tracks lead all the way home.

Le réveillon

together,
eyes, cheekbones,
the shape of the left pointer finger
rhythms buried in each cell
coming together and dancing
as family

the wondering
of what I'll look like older decided
the knowing of where and when I'll cry
at a perfect colour, a fiddle song, a tree standing alone
my words flow as his hammer
as his chisel as her music
watery-blue eyes search mine
as we speak our French
to each other
it's not so much what we say
it's the reassurance
that others speak like you

Raoul, my little one, remember that. You are never alone. Never. You will have me, and all our family, with you always.

x Rubis

Today is my birthday. I am fifteen years old. Marc has given me a black, heart-shaped stone with a hole pierced right through. He said that his love did that, pierced the stone so that he could put a thong through it and I could wear it in the hollow of my neck for always. To remind me that he loves me and that he will be with me, always. I will never take it off.

Marc's brother, Mathieu, has given me this little book to write in. He knows I like to draw and write down things. I think he's a little in love with me. But that's too bad because I am a woman married to a man and already there is a baby asleep in the cradle beside me.

Someday I will give this to you, lovely Raoul. Asleep there in the cradle your father made for you. You should know about these things, things that happen when you are without a care in the world and all the world is a breast!

Or perhaps I will give it to my daughter, who I know will also come into this cradle. I have seen her in my dreams.

I used to think that everyone could see things in their dreams, or standing wide awake. I thought that everyone saw the colours around themselves and heard the whisperings of those passed over and those not quite born. But they don't. I have learned that not everyone wants to know what I see. Unless it's good news, they don't want to know at all.

But I can't stop it when it comes and then I have to tell people about their dead cows or their rotten net or the death of a loved one. Good or bad, I have to tell them.

People here were more than happy when they found out I was a ramencheur, that I could pick herbs for their sicknesses, heal bones, stop fire in a burn, clear up bleedings, and act as a mid-wife, but they aren't too sure about the messages I hear and see.

So I will dream to myself and sing to my baby and love my husband. And pray that all will be well with our little family. Happy Birthday to me!

x Rubis

Alternative/ Folk Medicine / Part 2

Course: Physiology and Human Anatomy—Doctor Bussière

Interview with: Philia (née Morin) Massie
                       Patrique Delphis Joseph Morin
                       Léo Raoul Joseph Morin
                       Marie (née Morin) Casavant
                       Léonie (née Morin) Trefflé
                       Clémence (née Trefflé) Casavant
Location: Talon, Alberta
Date: April 1961
Interviewer: Phélice Trefflé—annotated notes

(Philia thumps on the table.)

Philia: Well, let's start. I'll talk, you listen.

Patrique: (teasing) Now, Philia, why did you ask us here if we can't talk
            too?

Philia: Yes, yes of course you can talk. Just not you! (firmly, pointing
            her chin at Phélice) We will start with this. (indicates an old,
            black exercise book) There are a lot of recipes and things in
            here. The recipes help us remember the stories, it's all tied
            together you see. You'll see.

Bonjour Philia!

*So good to hear from you. I wondered where you had disappeared to. Of
course I know how to make Tête au Fromage, but it is all from memory.
Other people might say this is wrong but it is all I know.*

*Papa used this recipe and he said he already have it in your Rubis book,
the red one, he says. Do you know what he's talking about? Hope it works
out for you.*

                                    Good luck! Be good. your sister, Annie

    hog head   *onion*
    tongue   *lightly salted water*
    heart   *a creux de main allspice*
    salt and pepper

Clean and scrape head. Remove eyeballs, ears, and nose, otherwise you can hardly stand to look at the thing! Wash thoroughly and saw into pieces (or half) depending on size of the head. Soak overnight in saltwater. Rinse.

Place head pieces in heavy roaster. Add water to almost cover. Simmer in oven until meat is very tender and leaves the bones.

Remove meat from bones and grind with other meat in meat grinder. Strain liquid. Put ground meat, liquid, onion, and seasonings together and simmer. (Add just enough liquid to make a nice consistency. It should be fairly thick.)

Freeze or can. Delicious on toast or sandwiches, with a hot cup of café blée!

Philia: Phélice, all this is Tête au Fromage stuff, from memory.

[ ] A picture of Baptiste and Evelyn Trefflé and their seven children.

Philia: This is la vieille Evelyn Trefflé, your mémère on your dad's side. She was Baptiste's second wife.

Little blonde girl
goes scuttling sideways while
behind her, on all fours
he goes at her rump, snarling like a dog.
Pokes her with a burning stick.
Throws a bloodied deer haunch after her through the door.

Her mother is worried at first
but the ones who stay
and the one in her belly crowd her
keep her busy as a fly on vomit.

Evelyn returns four days later,
with a guy from the camp
cradling the haunch filled with maggots
singing to it
as to a baby.

"Auprès de ma blonde, qu'il fait bon, fait bon, fait bon.
Auprès de ma blonde, qu'il fait bon dormir."

Her father figures he can do what he likes to her now

she doesn't talk much.

She knows what happens to fresh meat.

Phélice: That was my dad's mom? Is she still alive? Which one of these
            kids is my dad?

Léonie: Phélice, you don't want to hear about that! You didn't come
            here to talk about old family gossip anyways. Didn't you come
            for the medicine? Just look for the medicine stuff. (riffling of
            pages) Here, how about this then, einh?

For persistent coughing and chest pain

Mouche à moutarde
1 tbsp. mustard
3 tbsp. flour
1 cup water or enough to dilute the mixture

Mix, heat to dilute. When mixture thickens, put on old cloth then put another
cloth over it on chest. Adult dose: 20 to 30 minutes. Will burn.

Ferme-toi
1 med. onion chopped fine
2 tbsp. brown sugar
melt honey to cover onions
Mix together, leave overnight. Take 1 tsp. at a time.

Quand elle a finia fini son travail, que la fièvre s'en aille.

x Rubis

Phélice: That's okay Mom, really, I don't mind. I want to hear about
            Dad's family. Baptiste, he was a healer too wasn't he?

Léonie: Oh, look! Here is a good one! Especially good for ladies . . .

Wrinkles: melt and stir together 1 oz. of white wax, 2 oz. of strained honey and 2 oz. of the juice from lily bulbs. Apply to face every night.

Cold sores: blow on east window as sun is rising for 4 days.

Clémence: They used to call cold sores les feux sauvages—wild fires. They said that it was from fire in your mouth, bad words you know? (laughter)

Patrique: Then Baptiste should have walked around his whole life with puss-mouth! He used to swear something awful! Especially when he was talking about la vieille Evelyn . . . He used to say: "Sleeping with that woman is like fucking knives, all bones and hard places." (guffaws)

I remember one time, we were duck hunting on Mystery Lake, near de Pierpont's place. Crazy place that was, einh Léo? We had been there the year before, looking to fish. We asked old man Pierpont where the lake was, heard there was big jack in those parts. He had brought us to that place. No lake, just a smelly slough and wild hay growing all over the place.

—Where's the lake? we ask.

He lights his pipe, tilts his hat back and scratches his balls through the pocket of his overalls.

—It's a mystery, he says.

We laugh at that one! That Pierpont, what a joker, einh?

No fish, no lake, lots of ducks though. So fall comes and we head back out to the place. Enough whiskey and café, tête au fromage sandwiches, and boudin to last the night and morning. Baptiste is the one who wants to come so bad, really. The wife, Evelyn, is having one of her bad spells. She had these spells of, I don't what, just quit talking for weeks on end, and then she'd turn mean. And then of course she'd start drinking.

Wasn't easy living with old Baptiste, I guess. Yep, he was a strange one that Baptiste. He was a "healer" too, him. But did it with a book as I recall, big black book with shiny ribbons all inside the secret parts. Did some good work for a bit there, but he was, ah, a little too fond of l'eau bénit towards the end there. He could play the mouth-organ and guitar and sang through his nose like a real cowboy. Always popular at house parties, I can tell you.

And he had bees in his pants for that Létourneau girl, remember? She was pretty and all that, but Christ sake's, she was fourteen! Baptiste still had kids at home, so we say roll your own Baptiste! Pretty funny, einh? Roll your own? Get it?

Anyway, he can't stop thinking about her. Makes cracks about her like she's really coming for him and all that. Okay, he's a good looker, no doubt about that. Tall, big muscles, and lots of black hair, but still we laugh. We laugh and tell him he should take her swimming in Mystery Lake, that's how real it is. Mystery Lake, ghost of a chance being with that girl. Ha Ha!

Well, as I recall, about January that year, Baptiste started acting funny. He played good for the réveillon at Casavant's, and for la Fête des Rois, but he seemed nervous, like a moose with ticks. He couldn't sit still and he got pretty hard on the kids. Reuville, your dad there Phélice, I think was one of the youngest ones left at home, einh? He ate the most of it I guess. (someone coughs) Clémence was probably living with Philia and Delphis at the time, einh, Philia? Louise, his oldest girl, was gone already. Anyways, a, a lot of bad feelings there . . .

So there he was climbing over a barbed-wire fence and he goes and dies. They say he probably caught his snowshoe trying to cross over the top and his gun got snagged up somehow and goes off. Blew his head nearly right off.

We wondered for a while about that, walking with your gun cocked, but that was Baptiste, einh? Gun cocked, pretty funny, einh? (laughter and protests from the women)

(thoughtfully) You know too, they say he stayed in that

snowdrift nearly three days before one of his own boys found him. He was way hell and gone from the farm, headed in the opposite direction. Maybe following a coyote or something. The boy said his dad was maybe a mile or two from Létourneau's place, but in the snow, blowing and all that, he probably got turned around. Couldn't find his way home. It happens some-times . . .

Phélice: Who found him? Was it my dad? Where is that picture again? How old was he when died? Baptiste, I mean.

Clémence: (muttering, almost inaudible) It was your dad who found him. Had a hard time dragging that body home, frozen so bad. Could have left him there for the coyotes for all I cared.

Léonie: No, we had to bury him. Bury him and end his foolishness. Létourneau girl indeed! Hmpf!

Philia: (pointedly) But burying him didn't end the foolishness, did it? The Petersons moved to Talon in the fall, Delphis renting them the old Trefflé place. Well, not the big house, the little one just down the road they had built for Louise, the middle girl, and her husband. That dough-head August Beaupré couldn't keep a job if you put it in a box for him. Him and Louise finally left town after his last job with the Co-Op. He was so drunk they couldn't find him for two days. Passed out in the storeroom behind the bolts of canvas and his head on the big cheese wheel. They say it was lucky he was propped up, he'd of likely drowned in his own vomit.

Anyway, the Petersons moved in. Into a house that had nothing but tears for mortar and bad dreams for insulation. I believe what happened to them had nothing to do with them, really, and more to do with the curse old Baptiste Trefflé put on the place. How can you fight something or protect yourself against something you don't even know is there? He was so mad at Louise and August that he swore no child would ever laugh in that house. No child ever did.

Louise tried, you know, to get pregnant. Because a woman with-out kids isn't really a good woman, I don't care who your husband is! But those two drank, fought like two cats in a bag, and never went to church. It caused nothing but trouble and bad feelings for the Trefflés and Beauprés alike. What can you do?

So, like I said, the Petersons moved in. Delphis figured with Baptiste dead and Louise and August gone, that the curse would be gone too. It wasn't. The kids didn't last more than a month before they burned in that fire. All three of them, three boys, in their beds of all places.

Shame, really. Seemed like nice people, not our kind, but decent anyway.

After the funeral the Petersons moved away. Evelyn said she felt guilty for what happened. We said it was her husband had said no kids could live or laugh there, not her, nothing to do with her. Truth is though, she could have taken the curse off. Or asked one of us to do it. It's easier to do when it's fresh. Some say she kept it on just to see what would happen, but I don't know about that. She's not mean. Just forgot, is what I think.

Patrique: (singing) Le forgeron rebat le fer, il bat le fer, il bat le fer. We forge our own destiny. (The floor boards creak laboriously.)

Patrique: Jésus! That can't be good. I'll have a look at that and try to tighten 'er up.

Philia: Bah! Forgeron? Non, it takes a woman to end such foolishness. Louise, knew how to stop the fires. She burned that house to the ground, with her in it. It was a blessing, really.

Phélice: Oh my God! Is that true? Did she kill herself? Did she really kill herself? Was there a curse? Can you do that?

Marie: Now, well, ahem. Well, yes, yes, I suppose there was. I mean, it sure looks like that, doesn't it? Louise Beaupré wasn't right in the head really, if you think about it. She was always a little off? Wouldn't you say? Clémence?

Clémence: She wasn't so crazy. You want crazy, look to my own brothers . . .

Phélice: But she must have been! I mean, to kill yourself. Like that, I mean.

Marie:	Funny what we call blessings . . . blessings can be tricky that way. Sometimes it looks bad but you still have to try to see the good side. We were always pretty lucky with the way things turn out.

One time, I am coming out of the post office buttoning my blue coat and the button comes off. A boy walks toward me tipped way back, nose pinched to trap the rich dark blood within. Some spills into his mouth when he twists to say my name. To be polite and all I suppose. He passes me; I touch him and smile, just need to say his name, out loud. He takes four steps past me. With my eyes I trace a cross from the back of his head to his heels.

He takes another four steps and straightens his back, tips his head forward, the bleeding stopped.

Sunlight glints off the air so clear it hurts my eyes. I begin the prayer, and remind myself to re-sew the button on my blue coat. Then that young boy yells; "Fucking witch!" Bless him, curse me . . .

Phélice:	So the healing can be done without the person's knowledge or consent?

Patrique:	Well, Brendan, our old neighbour, wasn't French so he didn't believe in any sort of healing stuff, I mean that guy went out of his way to not believe, so we sort of taught him a thing or two . . .

We're butchering chickens one day, me and your mon oncle Léo there, and Brendan is buggering about. His Evil watching, drinking whiskey, making fun of our accents.

—Come on 'broders! 'Eal dis shitter! He whacks the head off a chicken, brandishing the torso above his head, dousing himself with blood. Thinks he's pretty funny that one.

—Don't screw around, Brendan. Patrique is a tiger-man when he's mad, Léo says quietly as he brings up another chicken, already hypnotized.

The stench of blood from those stupid birds always gave me a headache, and when I get a headache, ôtes-toi du chemin bon-homme! I look hard at Brendan through my cigarette smoke. I come up behind Léo and growl,

—Okay Brendanassole, chop de 'ead off.

Léo doesn't even look at me, just lays the bird on the block. Brendan roars and swings with a vengeance.

I close my eyes, more to keep the sun out of them than any-thing, and say the prayer.

The head falls off the stump, lands in the dust. I open my eyes and Léo holds the body up by the legs to show us. Held it there, pink skin gleaming beside bone. Nerves all jumping, shriveling in the heat. I look close. There's one drop of blood from the neck, just hanging there, like a big, fat red tear. I know nothing else will come out of that bird. The blood is shored up behind prayers, like it should be, like it always did, when I asked it to, back then.

I hear a magpie laughing in a tree.

I light a smoke, spit loose tobacco where the blood should be.

—Bon pour les cochons. Can't eat de meat if de blood don' come out. God did dat, little man. Imagine what He could do to you, standing dere, I say in the heavy way of talking that Brendan thinks we talk like.

Brendan walks away, back towards the house, doesn't say a word. Léo throws the carcass after him. It thumps him in the back, and never even left a stain. We laugh so loud. Feels good, like a prayer going down. And Jésus, my headache was gone!

Léo: Headaches? Yes, this family has headaches. We all get them, les feux de l'enfers. My little girl there, Marie, had bad headaches even as a little baby. Louise and I would watch as she banged her head against the crib bars. It was pitiful, really. Nothing we could do would help much either, no offence Philia.

Louise asked me once, just once, to see if I could help her. It nearly killed her that time so I never laid hands on her again. Marie went deaf. I am ashamed to say that.

These things, the ramenchage, for some reason never works on the family. It always gets mixed up. Mixed up and wrong. I don't know why. It wasn't a good thing, what happened, and it's all because I tried to help her headache . . . I never meant to hurt her. It doesn't work on family. I nearly killed my own daughter.

Marie: Oh Dad! Honestly sometimes . . . (she laughs) You never killed me; you didn't even come close. Takes more than that to kill a good Morin woman. So I'm a little deaf, so what? It cuts down on the noise and gossip I can hear, that's a good thing.

Phélice, let me tell you what happened. Dad's right, I always had bad headaches as a child. It was like lightning in my head, like knives of fire. I couldn't breathe, it hurt so much, and thank Blessed Marie we didn't have electricity back then. All that light would have finished me off for sure.

Mom used to put me in the bedroom with the curtains closed and a big thick quilt over top so no light could get through. Diane would come in and sponge my head with a cold cloth, and dump out the chamber pot I used to throw up in. She is a good sister that one! I don't care what others think . . .

I was about three or four I think when it happened. I remember that day so clearly. It was summer, right Dad? There was a big storm brewing. It had been so hot for so long. We all were looking forward to some rain. I remember because the day before I was sort of feeling sort of sick. I get like that when the weather is going to change. Mom had me put on that little blue straw hat when I went out to work in the garden. I loved that hat. It had a little scarf-type tie made of the softest . . . oh well, never mind that.

The headache started like they all did, sly and shy at first, little licking flames warming my brains and then BANG! Full blown like a storm. I felt a little better every time I threw up. This time was different, I guess, because I had the headache and some kind of infection in my ear, so they said later. Every time I vomited my ears would plug up more and more and more until I couldn't hear clearly anymore. But we didn't know that, about the infection I mean. What did I know about that? I was just a little child, and I was sick, like usual I thought. The doctor later told Mom and Dad there was a lot of scar tissue in there from the eardrum bursting.

Dad, we didn't know. How could we know? The fever wasn't big enough to tell us anything anyway until, well, way after. And what with the thunder and lightning that night, well, you guys already had your hands full.

So I'm laying in bed and trying not to breathe or anything, watching the fireworks behind my eyes. Dad and Mom are talking in the kitchen. I can hear them, but I can't make out what they are saying.

Then Dad comes in. And Mom holds me up and Dad does the prayer; I see his lips moving and I feel better. The pain is still there from my headache but the drumming in my ear stops at least. Dad asks me if it's better and, quite honestly, it was. Only the familiar pain of the headache and even that is slowly ebbing.

See, what Dad did was take away the pain. That's what he does, he takes away the pain from infections and stuff in the blood. Then the infection can clear itself with fever or antibiotics from the doctor or whatever. We didn't know it was infection. It felt better, that's all I know.

The infection just sort of kept on in there because we didn't go to the doctor. I got over the headache and went about my business, well, whatever business a little child can have! I was very glad my dad could help me.

The eardrum burst about, what, two or three days after that. Felt like my ear was peeing or something, warm and liquid feeling all down my neck. I had had a fever but not bad, and not hot enough to worry my parents or put me to bed. I guess that's what Mom and Dad thought it was, just me taking my sweet old time about getting over the headache.

I couldn't hear anything out of that ear ever since. And the other one is a little foggy too. I am not all deaf. I am a little hard of hearing, that's all.

Oh yes, I still get headaches. We still call them les feux de l'enfer, hell fires.

[   ]   Léo holding a stout, white-coloured branch in the shape of an Y.

Marie: Did I ever tell you that I could find water? Mon oncle Patrique
          and Dad could too. They took me along with them when I
          was just a girl and I found out that I could do it too. But most
          people liked having a man do that sort of thing. Seemed more,
          what . . . more true? More serious?

          Anyway, after Dad couldn't do it anymore, he would call me
          over and I'd walk along with him. Tell him where the water
          was hidden. He had that stick, see? And he would hold that
          stick straight out. And then, when I told him where the water
          was, he would make the stick go down, real slow. It was the
          only time I ever saw you lie, Dad, and enjoy it! Pretty good
          trick really . . .

          Oh, yes, we laughed when people wanted to borrow that stick!
          It wasn't in the stick at all, of course . . .

End: part 2
Qwiktype Typing
175 St – 131 Avenue,
Edmonton, Alberta.

Phélice reaches behind her and unplugs the extension cord they had rigged
up to work the tape player.

—Well, I guess this is a good start for my paper. Thank you for the medicine
recipes and the stories. I have a lot more questions but it's getting late and
I have to get an early start back to the city tomorrow. You know, she says
quietly, looking at Philia —that there will be a lot more questions from
Doctor Bussière too, once I get this all typed up, einh? No one is ever going
to believe this.

Philia smiles at her.

—Just tell them your family is a bunch of drinkers. In the middle of the afternoon no less, grunts Patrique from the back door, rising stiffly.

Léo shakes the bottle of Five-Star that appeared on the table during the afternoon and mimes drinking, his Adam's apple bobbing.

They all laugh and the tension evaporates. Rising from the table, the women begin to pile plates, cups, and cutlery. Léonie picks up a stack and motions to Phélice to do the same.

—Non, non, leave it, scolds Philia, —I'll need something to do with Clémence this afternoon. Go on you two, go on and finish your visit. And Phélice, why don't you leave that machine here for a while? We might remember more when you're gone.

Léonie pulls a pale-blue nylon headkerchief out of her sweater pocket, turning to the small mirror near the door to watch Phélice explain the workings of the tape recorder to Philia.

Marie and Léo gather into their coats, and make their goodbyes, kissing everyone on both cheeks, one for the angel on your right shoulder and one for the devil on your left.

Patrique is sure he has found the loose board and promises Philia to come back tomorrow and fix it.

Philia brushes his offer for help away with a sweep of her hand. —My old house creaks, Patrique. If you fix one board, another will act up, you know that. Let it be for now. It doesn't bother me. I like the company.

A board creaks loudly and Philia stamps her foot down on the offending floorboard.

—See that? she says darkly. —My house likes to talk, that's all.

Patrique laughs, puts on his hat, and heads for the car.

Before Phélice leaves, Philia hands her a brown grocery bag.

—What's this, Mémère? she asks.

Peering inside the bag she sees the two small exercise books, the same red and black ones Philia has gone through today.

—Take them, Philia says gruffly. —I already know how to make Tête au Fromage, you are just learning. You'll need the recipes because, she looks pointedly at Léonie, —some things are more complicated than your mother would have you believe.

She kisses Phélice twice on both cheeks and gives her a fierce hug.

Léonie sniffs and tightens the scarf around her head. She does not kiss her mother goodbye, just gives her the look, the "we'll talk later look." She doesn't know why all this old history has to be dug up. Phélice has done just fine up to now without having to open up those damned books. Those crazy stories about Rubis and healing nonsense and . . . Léonie shudders, has Philia written anything in there about Reuville?

Léonie looks down at the floor; she can sense something. She crosses herself quickly and steps outside. Phélice descends the porch steps after her mom, into the rain. She is startled when a fat black fly flies directly into her face.

The kitchen door slams shut.

Clémence thinks about inheritance—

Maman Evelyn's voice is tired and short
she stirs a brown onion sauce
for-fish-Friday-an'-l'Abbé-is-coming-tonight
"melt some butter to brush the bread
set the good dishes
and let GO of the cat"
Reuville turns to see me
pushes his tongue out
between pulled lips
I laugh too loud

Papa Baptiste burns across the doorway

heaves the kitchen
hurls a nest of swears at the crucifix
ready now to lay hands on something

my arm disappears under his fingers
and I'm kneeling

a head full of storm
and scared
sharing the closet
with the Diable in me

▨ Talon 1931

–CLÉMENCE – MARIE – EUGÉNIE – TREFFLÉ. Baptiste stands in the
yard and bellows her full name.

Inside Clémence and Léonie huddle together in the rocking chair near the
stove. Philia brings out another quilt and wraps it solicitously around the
two of them. She pats Clémence's skinny shoulder.

–Don't worry, she soothes. –Delphis will take care of this. It's no concern for
you, chouette. She brushes a stray hair from Clémence's tear-stained face.
–You just sit here and rock old Mademoiselle Léonie for a while, all right? She
gently tilts Léonie's face up to look her in the eye. –And you Mademoiselle,
not a word, do you understand? Stay with Clémence and don't move.

Léonie stares back up at her mother. –Oui, Maman, she nods vigorously,
places a thumb in her mouth, and leans back against Clémence.

–All right then, Philia says, –good girl. Both of you, quiet now and stay put.

She pulls on her coat and joins her husband at the door.

–I don't like this Philia, he mutters, I don't like this one bit. The man may
be drunk but it is not right to . . .

Philia arches her eyebrows and casts a sidelong glance towards the girls.
–You are right Delphis. I don't think it is right to have snow at the tail-end

of April either, but there you go. Some things we have to deal with, don't we? A lot of things don't make sense right now, do they? She challenges Delphis's steady blue eyes with her own. —Maybe M Trefflé can help us understand what is going on, einh? Do you think?

Delphis shakes his head wearily and asks, —Are your brothers around today?

He pulls open the door and peers out.

—Yes, I think so, I do believe they will be here soon. I lit the lantern in the north bedroom.

She gives the two girls one last warning look and gently pushes her husband outside into the swirling snow.

—Why did your maman light a lantern in the middle of the morning? asks Clémence, her face resting alongside Léonie's.

—It's a message for mon oncle Patrique to come over. Mam lights the lantern and he comes over.

—Oh, that's good, says Clémence absently, listening instead to her father, now bellowing curses at Philia.

Suddenly, the swearing stops.

Léonie snuggles deeper into the chair. —Mam and Papa will take care of this now, she says confidently. —Mam helps when, when people are struggling. Some people in pain and misery swear a lot you know, she confides, repeating her mother's long-standing explanation.

—Yes, I suppose they do, says Clémence, straining to hear something, anything to tell her what is going on outside.

She makes to get up out of the chair, but Léonie chides her.

—Non, Clémence. You stay here. Mam said.

—But I just want to . . .

—Mam said, repeats the little dark-haired girl, knowing full well the weight of her mother's words.

So Clémence settles back down on the chair and the two of them begin rocking. Léonie hums softly.

Outside, Baptiste stands, hands on hips, in the middle of the yard. His hair snakes wildly and his dark eyes glisten with a dangerous rage. To Philia he seems to be glowing white-hot in the midst of all the snow and wind, as if drawing strength from this freak storm.

She buttons her coat and moves closer to her husband. On the porch they are at least marginally sheltered from the storm. Philia glances nervously up the road. Where is Patrique anyway? Delphis is talking to Baptiste, telling him Clémence has been sick, that's why she came here in the first place, asking him to go home and to come back later when tempers have cooled off a bit.

Baptiste roars with drunken laughter. —Isn't this cool enough for you? he shouts.

He throws his head back and lifts his arms wide, embracing the storm. He turns two complete circles, laughing uproariously. Then he spots Aurore, Patrique's daughter, struggling up the driveway. A shawl covers her head. She doesn't see him standing there.

—Aurore! screams Philia. —Go back, child! Aurore! Run!

Aurore lifts the shawl from her head, a small puzzled smile blooming on her face. She raises a hand in greeting to her aunt. She freezes. Who is this running towards her?

Baptiste catches her around the waist and pins her roughly against him. Aurore screams painfully and struggles to free herself. Baptiste tightens his grip and drags the whimpering girl towards the porch, yelling at Philia.

—Philia! Hey, bitch, I'm talking to you. We trade, einh? We trade—flesh for flesh.

He shakes the sobbing Aurore roughly. —Come on now, you see it's a fair trade. What do you say? Fair, einh? Hey, Delphis, this baby-slut any good?

He barks a laugh and bends to crush Aurore's open mouth with his own. She gags and struggles in vain to keep her face as far away from him as she can.

—Ma tante! she sobs, —Mon oncle Delphis! Help me! Please help me!

Delphis roars and leaps off the porch towards them.

Philia clutches her coat at the throat and whispers the quickest prayer.

Baptiste howls in blood-curdling agony. His legs buckle. He falls heavily. Aurore disappears under the weight of his body. Delphis kicks Baptiste off the girl and rolls her, sobbing and gasping, into his arms. He picks her up and swings another powerful kick at Baptiste's rib-cage.

—Go home Baptiste, he growls through clenched teeth, and he strides back to the porch.

—You Jésus-fucking, priest-licking WHORE! Baptiste roars, rolling in the snow, clutching his leg in agony. —How dare you do this to ME! he screams, his voice breaking.

—Go home! Or I'll break your other leg, says Philia, clutching the porch railing, her neck muscles bulging. —Go home Baptiste, you're drunk. Go home and leave us alone. You have done enough harm. Enough, I say.

—You say? he hisses. Ah bien tabernacle de femme . . . I will tell you when it is ENOUGH!

Baptiste draws himself up. He raises his left fist at the house. He closes his eyes and slowly opens his hand.

From inside the house, Clémence screams.

Talon 1961

Phélice sits at her mother's kitchen table. She has neatly boxed and labelled her reels from this afternoon and places them inside the shopping bag with the books Philia gave her as she left the house.

She hefts the red book thoughtfully in her hands. What recipes, what mysteries and miracles are here in this book? she wonders. I wonder if Rubis ever thought that her words would be read some hundred years later? She sighs, I wonder if she would like me? Mémère Philia says we have the same hair, me, her, and Rubis. Would that be enough for her to like me, this Mémère who died so long ago? Was it a curse, like Louise suffered through? What really killed her? Was there nothing in her life worth living for? Children, husband . . . husband, she smiles and places the book back into the bag.

Léonie's silver-rimmed glasses flash with the up and down rhythm of her rocking.

She used to be a formidable woman, thinks Phélice; she used to be taller and I used to be so scared of her. Now look at her. She has grown so old in the last year. Spends more and more of her time just sitting and rocking in this kitchen, doing her crochet.

She really needs someone around here. Someone who can come in every day and look after her or well, okay, maybe not tie her down and force-feed her soup, but some company, something. It's not healthy for someone to spend so much time alone, Phélice thinks, knowing that she won't be able to be here much this summer.

—Mom?

—Hmm?

—Mom, are you lonely?

—What?

—Are you lonely. Don't you get lonely just sitting here by yourself all the time? I mean, wouldn't you like someone . . . I just thought that, well, I saw how everyone was today, together, you know, and mon oncle Patrique helping out and ma tante Clémence helping Mémère with the cleaning up, and I just thought that you might like to have someone, I don't know, living with you, to help you out sometimes.

—Phélice, says Léonie calmly, —I have you to help me out when you come in from the city and I really don't want any of that bunch coming in here and snooping through my drawers, telling everyone what I eat and what I don't eat or how dirty my cupboards are. Non, merci ma belle. I have had enough of them meddling in my life to last a lifetime! Merci quand même.

Léonie stops rocking and sits perched on the end of her chair, face tilted towards the fridge.

—What is that smell? Can you smell something? Like milk gone bad?

Squinting, she makes out the outline of someone standing next to the fridge.

Phélice ignores her mother's last words. She is used to Léonie doing this, pretending she can smell fire or soured milk or that she can see something, anything to interrupt a difficult conversation.

—But you had a good time this afternoon, didn't you? You still liked being with them all don't you?

—Non, actually I did not like this afternoon. You know I hate talking about all that old stuff, and Philia, when she gets on her high horse and gets going, well, it gets on my nerves, if you want to know the truth, snaps Léonie, putting down her crocheting and removing her glasses. —She treats me like a thirteen-year-old girl, hmpf! I hate that when she makes me feel like that . . .

She pinches the bridge of her nose, as if it pains her, and closes her eyes to the shadowy figure moving closer to the table.

Phélice is unsure about how to take the conversation back to her plans for the summer. Her mother seems so touchy all of a sudden. She chews on her already ravaged fingernails.

—Ah Phélice, I'm not mad at you, sighs Léonie, rubbing her eyes. —I just, I'm just too tired to argue right now chouette. I think I'll go to bed now, she smiles wearily, rising from the rocking chair and putting her hand on Phélice's shoulder.

She looks up at the ceiling, puts her glasses back on her face, and squints. Who is that?

—Mom? Phélice reaches for Léonie's hand. — Mom, I'm getting married.

Léonie's attention snaps back to her daughter. —What? Married? To who? Not that Pierre de Champlain, I hope. You are crazy, you hardly know that boy! Why, I've only met him once before and we have never even met his parents. Non, Phélice don't be crazy, this is much too soon. I won't allow it.

—Mom, Mom, calm down, Phélice twists from her chair and stands facing her mother. She puts her hands on her mother's arms. —Mom, look, I just thought I should tell you before, well, before we actually do it. We've sort of been living together now for the last six months and are thinking of going to Winnipeg this summer, for a couple of weeks. We'll probably get married there. See, his folks . . .

—What? You're shacked-up? Phélice, have you no shame? No pride? snaps Léonie.

—Shame or pride, Ma? Which is it, Ma? Can I have both and still be a good person? A good, French, Catholic girl? mocks Phélice, knowing she is treading dangerously. Her mother hates being corrected. The conversation is not going at all like Phélice had hoped it would.

—Shame on you, Phélice! Shame! This is not a thing to joke about. She points an accusing finger at her. — How will I ever explain this to Philia? Léonie moans, wringing her hands.

—You just said you didn't want any of "that" bunch in your life, Mom. Well, maybe I don't want them in my life either. After you tell them that Pierre and I have lived together, there will be no one to give me away. Or maybe they will all want to stand in line and give me away, one by one. Phélice glares at her mother, her voice tight. Cruel.

Léonie looks as though someone has slapped her in the face. She is too well acquainted with the idea of banishment to take it lightly.

She whispers, —Is that what this is all about? You want your family to turn their backs on you? You would run all the way to Winnipeg to find a new family? Are you stupid, Phélice? You can't trade families like that. The de Champlains are there for their own, not for you. They will always be there for their son, not for you. Never for you. You will never have a tie to them, no blood tie. You cannot. You will not have children with that de Champlain.

—Oh Mom, come on! Phélice throws her hands up in frustration. —For Pete's sake! We haven't even talked about having kids yet. We might plan for a family later, but Jésus. You call what this family does caring? Loving? Jésus, I don't even know my own family. You never talk to me about my dad. I find out bits and pieces from conversations like today and that's all. And then you try to shut them up every time they start talking about him. You call that caring? You call that loving? I pray that the de Champlain family isn't as loving and caring as this one! she snorts.

—I never said you couldn't ask questions about your father, says Léonie.

Phélice gapes at her mother then laughs, —Oh right, sure Mom. I can ask questions, I just won't get any answers, right? Oh that's beautiful, just beautiful, Mom. Phélice shakes her head in disbelief.

—Phélice listen to me. You go ahead and marry this de Champlain. I can't stop you. But you mark my words . . .

—What Mom? What? That my marriage will turn out as shitty as yours? taunts Phélice.

—Mark my words, you won't have any children with this Pierre and they will hate you for it. Léonie walks away from Phélice, heading towards the hallway.

—Why do you keep saying that? What do you think, because I have a club-foot like yours, I would be too ashamed to birth one? You make no sense! Not everyone in this world hates people with a clubfoot, Maman. Not everyone believes it's a sign of the devil, bellows Phélice. —Only this particularly charming, loving family!

—It's not this family! It's not this family at all, ma fille! I was talking about your father's family. You want to talk about loving and caring families? Then let's talk about the beautiful breed that you seem so in love with.

Léonie stomps back to the table and sits down heavily on the straight-backed kitchen chair, directly under the shadow she knows now must be her husband. Why else is Phélice acting so hateful?

Phélice crosses her arms and stares down at her mother. —What are you talking about? Did the Trefflés make fun of you? Are you afraid Pierre's family won't accept me because of this? She slaps her twisted foot. —Is that what all this is about Maman? she asks stiffly. —How stupid do you think they are? Not all families . . .

—Non, you are right Phélice. Not all families hate le pied bot, not all of them. But in French-Canadian families . . .

—Not the de Champlains, Phélice insists stubbornly. This is the sixties Mom! Only here in Talon does time stand still. Everywhere else, it's 1961!

—Phélice, I am trying to tell you about your father, about his family. You wanted to know about them so maybe I will tell you a little about what it was like . . . for me to live with them. And maybe you'll see why the de Champlain's aren't so different from all us after all. Why Pierre is just like . . .

—Don't, Mom. No, I won't listen to you when you talk like this. Phélice puts her hands over her ears. —You said yourself that you have only met Pierre once so you can't possibly know anything about him, okay? He loves me and he is a musician and that's all you have to know. That's all I know, that he loves me Mom. He LOVES, me. Poor, pitiful, ugly Phélice. Someone besides a bunch of dried-up old people loves me!

Phélice kneels down in front of her mother, puts her hands in Léonie's lap. —Maman, someone loves me. Be happy for me, okay? Just please, be happy for me?

Talon 1929

—Do you love him? asks Marie. The two sisters are getting ready for bed. Marie combs out Diane's long black hair. She faces her so that she can see her lips move.

—Love him? Of course I love him! I don't care what Philia says, I'm not a . . . a slut, Marie! I love him and he loves me. He even said so. And we are not staying here, oh non merci! Stay with this family? No sir, not us, we are on our way to British Colombia and the mills up there in the north. We have plans, you know. Oh yes, big plans, she says with confidence.

—What about Paul Poisseau?

—What about him?

—He'd marry you. He loves you. He even said so! And then you wouldn't have to leave or anything.

—Paul Poisseau, that little boy? Honestly Marie, that boy is so tied to his mother, the cord is still wet.

—But he would be a good provider, says Marie, imitating her father's deep, slow voice.

Diane snorts, —Yes, a good provider and at least I know he would never run away, she finishes bitterly.

Marie puts her hand over her mouth. —Oh, Diane! What a mean thing to say!

Diane waves her hand dismissively, much like Philia's wave this afternoon, thinks Marie.

—He is a cripple, Marie. It's not a mean thing to say, it's the truth and that's all there is to it. His leg stayed like a bird's femur after the accident, no matter what Philia and the others did. He limps around that store like a dwarf, sniveling and cowardly, like his father, but uglier.

Marie stifles a laugh, —Yes, and Madame Poisseau is the queen of the dwarves, einh?

—Queen of cue-de-poule, more likely. Can you imagine marrying that family? Having her for a mother-in-law, with her pointy mouth aimed at you all the time? It would be enough to swear off having children, in case they turn out like her.

—No children, ever, echoes Marie, suddenly sobered by the realization that her twin will have a child. —After this one, of course. She sighs heavily, —What are you going to do?

—I don't know, Diane confesses, taking Marie's hands into her own. —Everything is going so wrong, so very wrong. Roland didn't seem too happy about the baby coming, I guess I don't have to tell you that. He said he was going to British Columbia without me. That having a pregnant girl along wasn't part of the plan. Said he had to get away before all hell broke loose.

She looks down at her hands and those of her sister, together forming a protection over Marie's stomach.

The floor outside their bedroom squeaks and the door slowly creaks open.

—Les filles? Léo, their father, peeks his head in around the door. —What are you two magpies gossiping about at this hour? he asks kindly, his eyes already black with whiskey.

—Nothing Papa, assures Diane.

—Nothing Papa, echoes Marie. —We were just thinking of going to see ma tante Philia tomorrow.

—Yes, to help her, with . . . things around the house, finishes Diane, not looking at Marie.

—Well now, that's a good idea, of course. But your chores here come first remember. Now it's late. Time for bed, he announces firmly, as though they are both still six years old instead of sixteen.

—Oui Papa, they say in unison.

He averts his eyes as the girls remove their housecoats and tuck themselves under the quilt. He approaches Marie's side first.

—Bonsoir enfant de Dieu, he whispers into her good ear and kisses her forehead.

—Bonsoir Papa, Marie whispers back against his cheek.

He passes a rough hand over her head and smiles. She smiles back, her eyes half-closed.

He crosses over to Diane's side of the bed.

—Bonsoir mon ange, he whispers and bends to kiss her as well.

He stops, noticing the glistening of tears caught in her hair. —Are you all right, Diane? he asks, terrified that she will say no.

—I am all right, Papa, she murmurs. —I just wish Maman was here, that's all, she says under her breath.

But Léo hears. He brushes her forehead with an unsteady hand. —Yes, I would like that too, but, but . . . he sighs heavily and turns to leave the room, taking the lantern with him.

At the door he turns and says, —Soon as you girls tidy up the house and get the animals fed, go on to Philia's. I know you need a woman around to, to . . . he shrugs. —You know, to talk to, I guess.

He hesitates, what is that smell? The room smells like warm pennies.

—Go to sleep now. No more talking, he says gruffly. He closes the door quietly.

Diane wipes her tears with the pillowcase.

Marie spoons Diane and whispers in her ear, —He's getting better at this, don't you think?

Diane presses against her sister's body and takes her hand. —Yes, she says in all seriousness, —yes, he is, I think. Marie?

—Hmm?

—Do you think I am keeping Maman from heaven? she asks in her baby voice.

—Non, says Marie in the same small voice they have shared since the crib. —Maman died and went to heaven so fast St. Peter's beard flapped in her wind! she giggles.

—You are right, of course, sighs Diane. —I just wish Philia had not said that though, it made me feel bad.

—Ah, Ma tante says a lot of things, but you know her. She didn't mean that, or the wanting to kill you either, she didn't mean that. Not really, anyway. She will help you, Diane, believe that. If she says she will help, she will. We have to believe that.

—Yes, whispers Diane, —we have to believe.

As she drifts towards sleep, she hears the sound of their father playing the violin. Roland also plays the violin, almost as well as her father.

Her father is playing sad songs tonight. They are pretty, but sad.

—Like me, she thinks falling asleep.

Nous avons dans les cieux
Une Mère bénie,
C'est la Mère de Dieu,
C'est la Vièrge Marie.

O Douce Mère,
à Toi notre amour,
Sur cette terre
Sois notre secours.

Protégé tes enfants,
Gardé notre innocence;
Conduis nos pas tremblants
Et sois notre espérance.

x Rubis

Léonie's eyes brim with tears and her voice is husky. —Of course, chouette, of course I am happy for you. I just want you to be careful about this, you know a Catholic marriage is forever. Forever, she mumbles, her eyes drawn towards a sound and a moving shape on the ceiling.

Buzzing angrily above them, butting against the fluorescent light, is a large blue-black fly. It struggles to free itself from the web it has blundered into.

Phélice wipes her eyes then looks up to see what Léonie is looking at.

—I guess even the flies know when it's time to wake up, einh, Mom? she jokes weakly.

Léonie says nothing. She frowns at the fly.

—Mom? Are you okay? Phélice rises from the floor. I'll kill it for you, she offers, already heading for the fly-swatter Léonie keeps behind the broom-closet door.

—Léonie stretches her arm out to stop Phélice. —Non, leave it, she says anxiously. —Just leave it.

—Mom, what is it? What's wrong? Are you scared? It's just a fly, laughs Phélice.

—Look, wait. Léonie is still looking up at the ceiling. She whispers, —Maybe the spider will get it.

She points to an enormous, dust-coloured spider slowly making her way towards the fly.

Mother and daughter watch with morbid fascination as the spider closes in on its prey.

—That's what I felt like married to your father, breathes Léonie. —I was the fly and he was the spider. She touches Phélice's arm.

Their eyes meet.

Phélice silently embraces her mother and they stay that way, oblivious now to the struggle going on above their heads.

The spider reaches the sticky part of her web then darts in and attempts to subdue the fly, to wrap it in her silver. The fly buzzes frantically and its frenzied movements repel the spider. A few seconds later, when the fly is quiet, the spider scuttles out a second time. This spurs the fly on and it manages to rip itself from the intended shroud. The spider hangs upside down from the end of her torn web for a full minute before drifting lightly onto the table. She will simply spin another web and catch the fly another time.

La tresse, finie

le 5 mai, 1961

Chère Phélice,

Found this after you left. I know how anxious you are to prove this healing business, and maybe this will help. It wasn't just your family, you know. There were lots who could help. Before doctors, who else could help?

Je t'embrasse, Tante Clémence

"The Bloodstoppers"
Margo Holden
Official Farmers Almanac
Because the topic had interested me, I've asked around the state of Maine for more information. I find all old people who have worked in the woods can tell of times when a bloodstopper has helped someone. I have also found that many young people have heard of it from their old folks and some claim to have bloodstoppers in their own families. One farfetched story concerns a grandmother on whom the family, and in fact, the neighborhood, depended. She had only recently died when one of the young children had cut himself. All efforts to staunch the blood seemed in vain. One of the family lamented, "If only Grandma were here now. How I wish she were here to help us." The bleeding stopped suddenly.

le 21 juin, 1961

Chère fille,

We forgot to give you these when you were down. Never mind about all that stuff I said. You can always come home if you want.

Je t'aime, Maman

Phélice pulls out two reels of tape labelled: (A) Philia, Talon, and (B) Pour Phélice. She carefully threads a spool of tape to check the interviews again and flicks on the machine. The red power light glows. She turns up the volume and heads for the shower.

A dust-coloured spider pokes her body from out of the register near the tape machine. She hurries across to the reel, then lingers at the top of the machine.

Philia's monologue stops, starts up again. The voice stops again. Women are singing.

Phélice stops the shower. She walks into the living room, clutching a towel around her. She stares at the tape player.

Mon tour va venir un jour
Ça fait pas rien, quoi tu dis
Tu peux m'quitter pour coursailler
Ben mon tour va venir un jour

T'es tous les soirs après quoi tu veux
Tu connais t'as pas bien fait
T'après m'quitter pour coursailler
Ben mon tour va venir un jour

T'en a un autre à ton coté
Et moi j'crains c'est ça qui s'fait
Tu m'as quitter pour coursailler
ben mon tour va venir un jour!

(laughter from the women, glasses clink)

—That's for you Phélice! laughs Léonie. Don't be mad that we are singing on this machine. You said we could use it when we remembered other things, so we are. Anyway, it was Mom's idea.

(protests from Philia, more laughter)

—We wanted to give you a little surprise this year, something you really needed. The leather coat is from me. This advice is from all of us, woman to woman. We couldn't do it with the men here. We are going to sing it, like we used to sing advice for people around here, says Philia firmly. —We are using your fameux "tate regorder" and it will sing it back to you, einh?

(the women talk)

— This one is in case Pierre ever comes to you with a pain. You come from a long line of ramencheurs, but sometimes it doesn't work . . .

(Marie begins to sing, almost mournfully and the others join in)

> Mon mari est bien malade
> En grand danger d'en mourir
> Il m'envoyit qu'ri' du vin,
> Le meilleur qu'y a dans Paris.
>
> Je vous aime tant, temps en temps,
> Je vous aime tant, mon mari.
>
> Il m'envoyait qu'ri' du vin
> Le meilleur qu'y a dans Paris.
> Quand j'arrive sur ces
> montagnes
> J'entendis sonner pour lui.
>
> Quand j'arrive sur ces
> montagnes
> J'ai entendis sonner pour lui.
> Je prends mon panier d'argent
> Vitement je m'en retournis.
>
> Quand j'arrive à la maison
> J'l'ai trouvé mort, enseveli.
> Je le prends par une cuisse
> Dans mon jardin j'l'entrainis.
>
> Je le prends par une cuisse

Dans mon jardin j'l'entrainis.
J'appela pigeons, corneilles:
—V'nez manger, c'est mon mari!

(the women hoot with laughter)

—Let that be a lesson to you and whoever messes with you, Philia says solemnly.

—A ramencheur sometimes has a hard time with their own family. But mistakes can always become food for the birds or the worms! Clémence adds cheerfully.

(the women cackle delightedly and clink glasses again, the tape hisses)

Phélice smiles as she watches the spool turn round and round. So they knew about her troubles after all. Not such a surprise really, not in this family.

Phélice stares out of her apartment window. Thoughts of chains, dead babies and mothers, swirl through her mind. Dead babies, healing is in the bones, dead babies, the dreams she has been having, all those dead screaming babies and women and mothers and a crystal fob spinning at the end of a length of white thread.

She dabs absently at the water that drips from her long red hair with the tip of the towel. Is it me? she wonders. Do I dream of my own babies who are as good as dead because they aren't born? Is it someone else's baby? Whose baby is crying?

She watches a spider sway in slow circles, suspended from the tape recorder by an invisible thread. Her first reaction is to crush it between her hands, but she hesitates.

What keeps us from falling? Phélice wonders. What cushions us when we fall? Where comes the strength to climb back up again?

The spider sways gracefully at the end of her thread. Outside the wind howls, begging to be let in.

Phélice drags on her cigarette. She exhales onto the back of a fat bluebottle fly buzzing angrily against the window pane.

I am dreaming

When I pack up my things and go
who will stud my eyes with stars?
Who will scarf my hair with clouds?
Who will sing me to the stones?
Whose memories
will rainbow my passing?
I will
be snow,
the raspy cough of crows,
wind from four directions,
and the day moon in her honeymoon slip.

And who will know me?

x Rubis

⊠ Edmonton, Alberta 1961

Phélice nods over her papers. She is tired. Tired of looking for and never finding what her professor demands she find to substantiate her claim that her family can heal. Science documents the "what." Others could tell her that they had seen the "what." But where was the why?

Nothing in the articles she pours over can really help her. Nothing in her courses for nursing is helping either. How the brain works, how skin reacts to stimuli . . . nothing to say why the healing occurs. Nothing about the kind of healing her family can do.

Phélice rubs her eyes impatiently. Angrily stubbing out her cigarette, she swears and stand up.

—This is all so pointless, she spits. —It's like, like walking around the house with a match when you really need a candle . . .

The cat looks at her, one eye open. He begins to clean himself with a nonchalance that Phélice takes as a personal insult.

—Get out! she growls, hurling a pillow at the cat. —Get out and take your self-licking self with you!

The cat yowls and springs from the patch of sunlight on the floor as if suddenly burned.

The candle hisses wetly on the table.

Phélice blows out the candle and slumps from the room, taking her journal and the bottle of wine with her. In the bathroom, she shakes out five aspirins and washes them down with the last of the wine. She groans and flops onto the bed, fully clothed, praying for sleep—

> Matthew, Mark, Luke, and John,
> Bless the bed that I lay on.
> Four corners to my bed,
> Four angels round my head—
> One to watch, two to pray,
> And one to keep all fear away.

le 10 décembre, 1961

Chère ma tante Clémence,

I should have never asked Pierre to have a baby with me. I couldn't have known about him having the mumps when he was sixteen. How could I have known? If I had known how touchy he was about that, I would never have brought it up. I keep losing track of what I can and can't say, what I should and shouldn't say. Maybe having a baby would have brought us closer together. It would have made his mom happy, I know that. Please don't tell Mom this. I'll tell her myself at Christmas.

I'm tired of this fighting. It's been hell since we got married. Maybe? No, definitely a good thing to not have a child with a child. A child, him or me? Or someone else?

You wanted to know if I was still having those dreams, well, yes I am. This morning I had the dream of babies in a bag again. The crying and screaming women (?) woman (?). There's a rape. There's blood and there is a sack stained with blood. I think it has to do with the Pierre thing. What do you think?

And then I dreamed of someone, me (?) pushed up against the wall of the shed back home. Someone had an airgun and they were shooting nails at me. Every nail going in, shiny black-blue-green, like those big fat flies, but it didn't hurt. When he was done though, I knew I was dead.

That's bad luck isn't it? To dream of being dead in your dreams? Doesn't that mean you are going to die? No, wait, it means a wedding, I think. You can never witness your own death. The shock would kill you! I remember you told me that once long ago.

Well, better go to class. Please don't tell Mom about Pierre, okay? *I really want to tell her my own way.*

Gros becs, Phélice

le 20 décembre, 1961

Chère Phélice,

Looks like you need the recipe for sore heads, les feux de l'enfers. Marie gave it to me. She says it comes from Rubis's book, but I don't know if you still have that old piece of junk anymore. Here it is in case you don't.

Take care of your head, chouette, it is the resting place of the soul. Use this little token to help you relax.

You aren't alone. Don't worry so much about those dreams. They are clear to me and will be to you too, later. See you at Christmas.

Je t'embrasse, Tante Clémence

Raoul my child, you suffer from headaches like your father before you. Here is what works: Eat 3 or 4 pickles, the real sour type or a big crunchy, ripe tomato. The acid is good for your stomach. Press on the inside of your wrists and the muscle under the web of skin on your thumbs, to keep from throwing up. Use willow bark or hawthorn-berry infusion for the pain. Stay out of the sun.

> *Infusion:*
> *Creux de main finely chopped and ground white willow bark and a pinch of hawthorn berry*
>
> *Pint of boiling water. Let the herbs sit for a good bit. Use a teapot to keep the steam in.*
>
> *Dose: cup taken three times a day.*

x Rubis

Phélice massages her temples and rubs her eyes. Where am I supposed to get bark, for Pete's sake? she thinks. I don't even know what hawthorn looks like!

Her eyes fall on the suncatcher Clémence sent her: a small piece of crystal in the shape of an elongated teardrop. It dangles from her hand by a short length of string.

It winks at her.

She blinks.

As it turns ever so slightly it winks at her again, catching the weak morning sun and sending it sharply back into the room. Phélice watches, open mouthed, as the crystal turns slowly, one revolution in each direction, then begins to move in a circular motion.

What was that? That movement. Where has she seen it before?

Her mind flips back to the article she read on diving, dowsers, using a pendulum. She shuffles through her papers and flings books aside until she finds the newspaper article:

Looking for gold, oil, or a way around a traffic jam? "If you can dowse, it's only limited by your imagination," says Dan Tips, who owns a sprinkler repair firm in Garland, Texas.

"If you feel the power of your mind, it's the strongest thing you've got. Don't just ask for water, or you'll get the bathroom pipes," Tips advises.

Skeptics love to poke holes in this stuff. Scientists say that dowsing has never been proven to their satisfaction. Some religious fundamentalists believe that dowsers are messing with dark forces best left undisturbed.

But none of the 100 or so people attending the conference seems perturbed. In the arid Southwest, it's as much a part of frontier lore as barbed wire and wagon trains.

"I grew up in the country, and dowsing for water was a given," says Stephanie Chisholm, a Dallas investment company secretary, "But I thought it was only for gifted people."

According to dowsers, their Y-shaped rods can react to the presence of whatever you're looking for (water, gold, your parked car) or indicate a yes or no answer to a question you ask out loud.

They can even work over a map, far from the actual site being dowsed.

For more complex tasks, many dowsers use a pendulum, a small weight suspended from six inches of string or chain. By the direction it rotates or swings back and forth, a dowser can deduce nearly anything.

Phélice remembers her mom holding a ring strung with white thread over the bellies of pregnant women. A circle meant the woman was carrying a girl. A back and forth motion meant a boy lay nestled in the darkness.

She sees ma tante Marie in her mind's eye, holding a ring or a pendant over her upturned hand, asking questions. If the answer was yes—a circular movement; no—a back and forth swaying.

Wait! Yes! That's it!

Taking a deep breath, she holds the suncatcher over her left palm. Is that right? Right or left? Does it matter? Can't remember, not important. Does this work? She waits. Nothing but trembling from her own hand.

Oh, right, a question. Um, ah, are you there? Come on, come on. Where are you? I know someone is there. Come on, show yourself. Help me.

She gives it a little shake. Nothing. She puts it down.

Frowning, Phélice lights a cigarette and watches the crystal on the table in front of her for signs of life. She prods it with the end of her lighter. Sighing, she picks it up again. The smoke from her cigarette travels along her arm, curls itself near her ear.

—Are you there? she whispers. —Are you there? she repeats, louder this time.

The crystal begins a slow circle, ever widening like ripples caused by a stone thrown into water.

—Do I know you? she says aloud.

The ornament swings uncertainly—yes, no, yes. Smaller movements— uncertain. Slowly, slowly. And then it stops.

—Ah shit! breathes Phélice. —Come on, dammit! What am I doing wrong?

The cat yowls from the living room. Phélice drops the crystal in surprise.

—Damned cat, she mutters picking up the string again.

She drops the crystal into the junk drawer and stubs out her cigarette. She goes to the bathroom, nearly tripping over the cat, who is ferociously eyeing a spider crawling purposefully along the vent.

—Stupid cat, she mutters, holding onto the doorframe for support, the soured remnants of wine threatening to spill up her throat.

The cat eyes her maliciously.

—What I wouldn't give to see inside your head for five seconds, hisses Phélice. —SSSSSSS! White noise probably, einh? SSSSS, she spits at the cat.

The cat stalks off towards the kitchen and another vent.

Phélice lifts her head from the toilet bowl. She hears the sound of violins. Can the wind sound like violins? Is Pierre playing the violin? She cocks her head and listens. No, Pierre is rehearsing at the university today.

She groans and pulls herself up off the floor. She heads back into the kitchen, intent on making herself a big strong cup of tea with lots of sugar. Can't find any hawthorn, may as well use sugar and tea. Always a good remedy for shock or hangover, she thinks.

Sipping from a mug that boasts, "Talon – Fête au Village 1960 – Vision – Courage – Heritage," she picks up the textbook she needs and makes her way to the couch. Something pokes her from under the couch cushion. She pulls it out. It is a book Pierre bought for her in the early days. What is this doing here? Squinting through the pain of her headache, she reads the inscription on the first poem:

To My Little Phélice—I hope this answers some of your questions. Never stop questioning, that's what I love about you. Gros bec, Pierre

Mr. Nobody
Anonymous

I know a funny little man,
As quiet as a mouse,
Who does the mischief that is done
In everybody's house!
There's no one ever sees his face,
And yet we all agree
That every plate we broke was cracked
By Mr. Nobody
'Tis he who always tears our books,
Who leaves the door ajar,
He pulls the buttons from our shirts,
And scatters pins afar;
That squeaking door will always squeak
For, prithee, don't you see,
We leave the oiling to be done

By Mr. Nobody.
He puts damp wood upon the fire,
That kettles cannot boil;
His are the feet that bring in mud,
And all the carpets soil.
The papers always are mislaid,
Who had them last but he?
There's no one tosses them about
But Mr. Nobody.

She shivers. It is as if someone has pressed a cool hand on the back of her neck. She goes back to the kitchen to find the crystal teardrop. She has another question.

Phélice waits until Pierre is settled in front of the TV. He is massaging his hands with oil of wintergreen, his new ritual. Says his hands pain him whenever he walks into the apartment. It is Phélice's fault that the place is so drafty. He needs to keep them warm and supple to play the violin properly.

He's moaning now as he fastidiously rubs more oil between his fingers, —I am going to end up a cripple because you can't remember to turn on the heat in this hole. Then what will I do? A fucking cripple and useless!

She tut-tuts from their darkened kitchen. —I'll take care of you, Pierre. I'll have a job soon and I'll help out more. Really, I will, and then we can move to a nicer place.

—You? he snivels, —you're a useless cripple now. How will you ever help me?

—I'll help you right now, she croons, coming into the living room. She offers him a mug of steaming liquid. —See? Tea for you, Monsieur. Herbal tea Margot gave me. She said that it . . .

—Margot? That dried-up, useless twat. Why would I drink anything she gave you? Take it away.

—Well, what would you like instead? I can make you something warm, it makes your hands feel better when you hold something warm. She leans closer to him, to brush the hair from his forehead.

His fingers suddenly grip her forearms. Her jaw clenches against the surge of pain. She wills herself to stay quiet, to keep from spilling the mug into his lap.

He pulls her menacingly closer, fingers digging deeper into her arms.

—I don't want fucking tea, all right? Make me a ponce. Think you can do that?

He pushes her away from him. The mug flips up and over, scalding her through her thin sweater, but it is Pierre who howls in pain.

—My hands! My poor, poor hands! He hunches over himself, cradling his now rigid hands in his lap and crying.

His hands look mottled because of the light from the TV, thinks Phélice. She watches in awe as they twist inside themselves, sinew and veins writhing, straining to prevent Pierre from making a fist.

—Phélice do something! This is killing me, he moans.

—I'll get you something, she whispers, I'll be right back. She picks up the mug from the floor and hurries to the kitchen and the little bottle she has stashed in her handbag.

I am at Mémère's. George Beaupré gave me a lift from The Corner. Said Mom was at her Femmes Chrétiennes meeting. Don't want to be alone tonight.

I'm gone from there. Out of there. He'll never look for me here. He won't dare come here. He'll wake up and well, then we'll see.

Mémère found the bottle of chloral hydrate in my bag when she went rummaging for cigarettes. I told her what I'd done. She didn't look surprised or anything. Just asked me if I thought 1,000 mg would be enough. "Enough for what?" I laughed. "I gave him two pills in his ponce, just to make him sleep a good long time. Time for me to get here, get safe. I didn't want to kill him, Mémère!"

She nodded slowly then made me a cup of hot chocolate with a whole Hershey bar.

It'll be all right now. She's downstairs, smoking and talking to herself. I'll have one more cigarette and sleep too.

Les filles de Talon

[   ]   Madelaine, Aurore, Marie, and Diane—two sets of twin girls—behind a long row of saplings.

If they survive, we will have protection.

Edmonton 1962

Phélice hums softly, her head bumping gently against Patrique's car window.

> Au clair de la lune,
> Mon ami Pierrot,
> Prête moi ta plume,
> Pour écrire un mot;
> Ma chandelle est morte,
> Je n'ai plus de feu;
>
> Ouvre moi ta porte pour l'amour de Dieu.
>
> Au clair de la lune,
> Pierrot repondit:
> Je n'ai pas de plume,
> Je suis dans mon lit.
> Va chez la voisine:
> Je crois qu'elle y est,
> Car dans sa cuisine
> On bat le briquet.

Patrique Morin is beside her. He smiles at his Phélice. His eyes take up his smile and holds it there, as a twinkle. Settling herself in the passenger seat, Phélice thinks he is probably her favourite uncle, always busy, always working or fixing things, and always ready with a joke and a good stiff drink.

See? she thinks. Already, he is reaching for a small silver flask from under the driver's seat. He winks at Phélice and unscrews the top with one hand.

–I'm glad you agreed to come with me to the airport, Phélice. An old man like me tends to get lost easy in the big city. A ta santé, ma fille! he says before swallowing a healthy mouthful and passing the flask to her.

–I think Mom and ma tante Clémence and ma tante Marie had enough on their hands today with all the planning without taking care of me too. Ma tante Diane and her Paul were coming in this afternoon from Calgary. They would all like some time to relax a bit before the funeral tomorrow. A ta santé, mon oncle Patrique, Phélice says before she too refreshes herself.

She puts the cap back on, fingering the engraved "PJM." —So, are you excited to see your daughters? she asks.

—Excited? Patrique looks sideways at her. —Well, yes, I am all tingly, he says in a high-pitched voice.

Phélice punches him playfully in the arm. —You know what I mean, she says, grinning. —When was the last time you saw ma tante Madelaine? And ma tante Aurore? They moved away so long ago, I don't remember them very well . . .

—Yeah, you were pretty young, I guess . . . Patrique checks his rearview mirror, flicks on the turning signal, and changes lanes before answering. —Get me a cigarette, will you Phélice? he says easily, slouched in the driver's seat, his left arm resting on the open window frame.

Phélice pulls her pack out and lights two. She hands one to her uncle. She loves his hands. They are weather-beaten to a tanned leather-brown all year long. Their blue veins stand out so clearly you can almost see the pulse of blood.

Patrique glances at his niece, —What are you smiling for? Just glad to get away from all the crying and arguing about whether to have potato salad or coleslaw, I bet, einh?

He stretches forward to turn on the radio.

Phélice laughs easily, —Just that your veins stand out so nicely it would be a cinch to draw blood from you. She turns down the radio. —Do you mind? she asks.

—No, but I can't hear it if it's that low, he says turning it up again.

—But I can't hear you talk if it's that loud, shouts Phélice.

—Then don't talk, mouths her uncle, turning it up yet again.

She wrenches the radio off. —If you think I'm going to sit in a car with you all the way to the airport and have to listen to Bev Munroe the whole time you are mistaken.

—Well, I guess I could always sing . . . and he launches into, "I fall to pieces . . ." his rich, baritone voice filling the small space between them.

Phélice joins in, shyly at first, sneaking glances at her uncle's profile, then sings with more gusto when she realizes that he is so into the song that he has forgotten she is there. The car is filled with their voices and the pain they both use to colour the song.

Patrique sighs, —They don't write 'em like that anymore, einh Phél?

Phélice nods, lost in her own thoughts.

Patrique glances at her. She needs a husband, that one, he thinks paternally. He pats her on the knee.

—Mon oncle, do you think love is like that?

—What do you mean, fille? he asks, lighting a smoke from the open pack on the seat between them.

—That people fall to pieces when love dies? Do people die of a broken heart, do you think? She lights herself a cigarette.

—Well, I think that would be rather messy, don't you? he says in mock seriousness. —I mean, people walking around, an arm falling off here, a leg there . . .

—What about the broken-heart business, do people die from a broken heart? Or let's say a husband dies, do you think the wife would die too, out of loneliness? She shifts in her seat, tucking her feet underneath her legs, resting her arm on the back of the seat.

She continues softly, —Or is it more like that song . . . "Mon mari est bien malade, en grand danger d'en mourir. Il m'envoyit qu'ri' du vin, le meilleur qu'y a dans Paris . . ."

Patrique visibly bristles at the words. —I was real sorry to hear about all that business with you and Pierre. I never liked him, if I can tell you that. He had crooked eyes, if you ask me.

138

—Thanks, she says dryly.

—Well?

—Well what?

—Are you thinking of dying or of killing him? Pierre, I mean, because of what happened?

—No! No, heavens no. No, that is part of my life that I don't want to live out again, but, but . . . she is surprised to find her eyes tearing.

—It's all over with, einh? Patrique pats her leg again and launches into, "I've loved and lost again. Oh what a crazy world we're living in . . ."

Phélice rest her head on the backrest. She drinks from the flask and, when her uncle is done singing, she passes it to him.

—Ah! That's the ticket, he says, wiping his mouth.

—So, she says after recapping the flask and slipping it under the seat.

—So?

—Does it happen? she prompts.

—Does what happen? he asks.

—Do people die from a broken heart?

—Oh, for Pete's squeak, Phélice, I don't know . . .

He shakes his head and Phélice thinks he will turn this into another joke. She is surprised when he begins talking in a low, serious voice.

—There are some people who feel more deeply than others, I suppose, and those people might die from a broken heart. There are lots of different kinds of pain, you know. And lots of ways of dying. Say your child dies, you die a little too. Or say someone loses his temper and hits one of the kids, or talks too hard to the wife, or hits her. Well, that's something you can mend, einh? Well, you don't die from that, he continues, looking at her from the corner of his eye. —But you could die a little bit each time and then one day, poof! It's just too much and you do die. Something dies, at any rate. Do you see that? Can you see that happening?

—Yes, I think so, says Phélice thoughtfully, relieved that she has someone to talk to this way. —But what I mean is a husband and wife . . .

—Yes, yes, I was getting to that. He runs a hand distractedly through his hair, smoothing out the corners. —That's what it was like for Aurore, he says. —She didn't die all the way when her Guy passed over, just a little. Just dead enough to keep her from the pain of living without him. They never had kids. Aurore was, ah, unable, and so Guy was her whole life. When he died, she did too, a little bit every day.

—That's so sad, I didn't realize . . .

—Yes, sad. A whole life wasted, really. Lucky for Aurore that Madelaine was there to help pick up the pieces. You won't know any of this because they left for British Columbia shortly after you were born. They weren't running away from you though! he jokes looking over at her.

 —Mom said ma tante Aurore went to Salmon Arm first.

—Guy had a job there. An uncle had a ranch and needed someone to manage it. They left Talon and set up there for a couple of years, then he was killed in a thrashing accident.

The very words "thrashing accident" conjures for Phélice the most vivid bloody images. Anyone growing up around farm machines knew the deadly combination of metal thrashing belts and the flesh of man. She shudders.

—Madelaine went there to help her out and never came back, finishes Patrique, flicking his cigarette out the window.

—Never? They never came back until now? I thought I remembered seeing them one Christmas.

—Visiting isn't coming back to live, Patrique says with unusual crispness. —They went away and they stayed away, end of story.

Phélice knows that tone of voice. Her mother uses has that same tone and sets her jaw the same way when the subject is closed.

—They should have come back after a while. Not right to have stayed away for so long. Could have come back. No one blamed them, Patrique mutters under his breath, scanning the parking lot.

—Blamed them? For what?

—For taking care of a bastard-pain-in-the-ass who shoulda died anyways, that's all.

—What? Who died?

—Looks like we're here. Come on, Phélice. Help me get those old ladies.

Patrique parks the car and pulls himself out of the driver's seat.

Léonie smokes quietly and listens as Phélice drags herself from bathroom to bedroom. She smiles indulgently at Phélice, who is swearing all the while.

—I did so pack those black jet earrings so now where the hell are they? Don't you ever clean anymore? My God! The spider webs in here could make a shawl! Mom? Do you have anything black I could wear with this dress? Mom?

Phélice pokes her head around the bedroom door, dressed only in a slip, her hair arranged in a braid at the back of her head.

—Mom?

—Hmmm?

—Aren't you getting ready? They want us there at nine right? She waves her bottle of Evening in Paris toward the kitchen clock.

—Doesn't take me as long to get ready as you, says Léonie, straight-faced.
—I've had years more practice.

—Would you like me to do your hair for you Mom? Phélice eyes her mother's stiff, grey curls.

—Non merci quand même ma belle, Léonie pats her hair. —I will just comb it out when you are done in there. Go on, go ahead, you get ready now. I will just finish my cigarette and slip on my dress when I'm done.

—Mom? Are you okay? I mean, will you be okay?

—Yes, yes, of course. The ladies from Les Femmes Chrétiennes are doing the meal over at Mom's and there'll be enough food left over to feed us for three days.

—Who will sleep here tonight? asks Phélice, swatting at a fly buzzing around the perfume.

—No one, just us, I guess. Marie will have Diane and Paul at her place and Clémence fixed up the spare room at Mom's for Madelaine and Aurore.

—Ma tante Aurore isn't feeling too hot . . . she didn't look so good when we picked her up yesterday.

Léonie flips through Phélice's notebook. —She's probably just a little tired. Travelling is hard on a person, makes you confused. She tends to lose her way from time to time anyway, that one . . . Léonie hesitates. —Tell me that never happened to you? she finishes, waving the book at Phélice.

—I know mon oncle Patrique told me . . . Oh Mom, don't read that! Phélice laughs uneasily, adjusting the shoulder-strap of her slip. —It's just dreams and things, it doesn't mean anything.

—Your mémère used to write in a book like this all the time. So did her Mémère Rubis . . . you doing the same thing now? asks Léonie, stubbing out her cigarette in the small, orange turtle ashtray, already filled with this morning's ashes.

—Maybe, shrugs Phélice. I like to write things down so I can make sense of them later. But it's not for you, okay?

She plucks the book from her mother's hands and tucks it back into her bag. —Now, come on, time to get ready, and she disappears into the bedroom.

When Léonie hears the swearing begin again, she takes the book out of the bag and lights another cigarette. She calls to her daughter, —I'm going to start a pot of coffee. Do you want some?

—Yes, that would be great, thanks.

Phélice's voice is muffled, like she has her head buried in the suitcase, thinks Léonie. She carries Phélice's journal to the kitchen counter and thumbs through entries as she prepares the percolator.

Voices fade to whispers.
When a child listens,
it is the deepest silence there is.

Listen to your heart Raoul. That's where God beats His Message.

x Rubis

SPRING 1961: INVENTORY OF MY SOUL

Crimson lines where lives dark spruce.
Slow-moving, deep-breathing slough creatures.
Moon,
sun,
stars cupped in the hand of robin-egg blue.
Smell
of scrub brush, juniper, saskatoons, sand, and blueberries.
Taste
of real cream: yellow, thick, and still warm.
Honey I crack with my back teeth from the wax crumbs Pépère offers from behind the beekeeper's veil.
Flowers
from the hen and chick cactus, creeping charlie on the north side of the house where the well was.
Smell
of burnt metal after pennies are crushed by a train in the early morning, while magpies worry the carcass of a gopher.
Smell
of wood smoke and gas.

SCALES

Could I be a doctor?
like Mémère was a doctor, like Rubis was.
My kitchen feels like an office.
Margot's sister sits and weeps into her coffee bowl filled with red wine,
"I'm okay with the fact that she'll die, but when?"

She blinks at me through streaming mascara.
I look away.
Play with my cigarette.
Feel the headache howling behind its door.

This mother rocks her girl child, stroking hair
soft down and long stray pieces.
Their eyes, pale blue and hollow from the smoke of
a dying fire.

The girl sucks her thumb and touches her mother. The mother's jaw is
crooked; she's lost, in total, as much as her daughter weighs. She doesn't
ask any more questions.
She's wagered her own life for the girl's. They sit,
perfectly balanced,
for now.

SUMMER 1961: DOORS OPENING

Margot has her wrist wrapped in a bandage
holds it close to her chest
tilts it like a box filled with broken glass

she approaches silently
stands in front of me
unwraps the burn   I feel an old door
                                             opening in my head

she asks if I can help her   I split in two

I touch her wrist   the vein in my

                    forehead throbs
                    rivers
                    memories
                    sky

one side blazes
asking for details, clucking in sympathy

                    pouring out
                    and over a wash of
                    yellow

one side touches her wrist again, turning it closer
lightly tracing the sign of the cross

                    it's a picture
                    of all the words

she smiles crookedly
and turns to leave.

"Thanks Phélice, she says, shyly, uncertain where the pain went.
"Don't worry, it won't hurt anymore," I say thickly, "and it won't blister."
She smiles again.

                    I remember
                    a prayer

When all else fails there is always this. Use salt pork to soak a foot when some-
one steps on a nail. Blow smoke into a sore ear. This is practical magic.

x Rubis

Dream, a man

see shoes, black boots, scuffed boots, brown boots
standing close

too close, shoes lift and settle
muttering
together then two behind and two ahead
grim face, Delphis, pulling me up, beside me, a gun?
eyes like ice, Philia, other side
poking and pushing mumbling

"Can't walk no faster woman, Jésus, Marie, Joseph! Where we going? Little
party? Little surprise?"

What? Here? This is bush, blackscratchy things

What? Pushing down, crunch, scritch scratch here

Hide?

"What, ME hide? No, not me, her! Make her hide, she's the Bad One."

Pushing down, gun butt close
come stand all close
see shoes, boots still
quiet now
no sound now

they stand close
no sound watch me watch my mouth
move my finger move

there is ice cold, cold so cold
there is hard break of bone breath of bone to stone cold hard break like ice
they watch me break
to ice smell earth face in the earth
break of stone can't move no breath can't breathe tight
so black-night cold cold so tight too tight stop can't fit split I am—

Now move slow now easy yes
easy water
follow smell
heat

find light

Now make wake
light moves
make hurt

sniff out hurt
feel hot cold   move

Dream, a woman's frustration

We scent her with oranges and warm pennies
We send her her secrets of the kitchen, the body, the mind

                she scribbles outside the lines We set
                she whispers into her bathwater
                and twirls a needle on a white thread above
                her belly

this child is Our child
Our ability to speak—

                she asks why the sky is blue
                and seeks the dark one

We offer dreams and magic
We sing family and blood ties—

                she sews them onto her coat
                and reads without pictures

I can hardly tell if I am awake or asleep anymore. If I am careful I can almost put a face to the dreams, to the voices. One of them is my mémère Rubis. One is, I think, my father. But why is he in such pain? He comes to my sleep after Pierre has raged against me. I go to sleep thinking I want to kill myself, end this miserable life. I have the two voices, arguing in my head–kill or be killed. What sort of thing is that? Phélice, 1962

Dream, a woman, on guard

We catch her as she falls downstairs
We comfort her for the two days she wanders without a thought
after she is flung from that bicycle

We entice her back to the body
with memories of bread and chocolate
when she dreams of the babies

We wave that truck into the ditch
so she doesn't hit
it

she is most work though when she falls

asleep
in the skulls of the dark one

there is an Evil there
and
its
humming

lulls Us

Calling the black dahlia

she finally answered the question,
what did it feel like
to be a conduit for the healing—
what was it like—?

in that profusion of
dandelion, clover, and creeping charlie
to be an exotic flower?

Mémère said,

"Je m'ennuie"

After the funeral they gather at the house. The food is placed on the table the men have dragged in from the kitchen to the living room. Philia's date squares are conspicuously absent. Everything else feels and looks as though Philia will come bustling in at any moment and take charge. She loved preparing the lunches after a funeral, everything so sweet and heavy, made you remember that you were alive.

Philia's rocking chair sits in its usual place of honour beside the stove in the sun-dappled kitchen. The bleeding-heart-of-Jésus picture and the black-and-brass crucifix hang over the arch leading into the kitchen. The United Grain Growers calendar, a pad of paper, the coffee cup filled with pencil stubs and leaking pens stands behind the black telephone on the corner shelf she had Delphis put up the day they got the phone.

Léonie is dry-eyed. A headache is gnawing her inside out. She stands beside the stairs leading to the basement. She has gone back to when she was a little girl inhaling cool, dirt darkness, shivering on the bottom step, feeling the smell of potatoes in gunny sacks, in a corner somewhere down there. Potatoes with ivory-pulp feelers, fingering the sides of the sacks, begging the wall beyond for sun and warmth.

There, alone, she thinks, when I squeeze my eyes till lights zigzag I hear laughter, smell sweat, salt, and warm rubber boots, see Mom's red nylon kerchief holding back curlers all-day Saturday, fingers lolling in the dirt, her laugh opening wide. No one laughs in French anymore.

Léonie thinks about where headaches come from—

I do not want breakfast
morning time makes me dizzy
in the corner where I sit shaking

I see Maman put yellow cream in her copa choklit
she bangs down my plate and points—"breakfast"
the cat furs my leg
wanting the white skin on my egg

the plate bounces twice
it hits the cat

it hits the floor
her hand hits my face
it does not bounce
and it hits my face

Marie opens the heavy curtains in the living room and checks on her coffee
percolator, gurgling on the extra card-table set up with cups and saucers
and the jam jar full of spoons. She sniffs. The smell of Philia's pipe tobacco
lingers everywhere, in the cushions when they sit, in the curtains, in the
small throw rugs she has scattered about to protect her floor.

Marie would much rather be at home, among her own things and smells.
Amidst the maelstrom of memories, she can simply look up and something
will catch her eye, will fish-hook a thought. She doesn't have to make up a
single new thing. Like stirring a soup and knowing you'll see the carrot,
potatoes, celery, onion, and an occasional blot of meat. Nourishing for the
old soul doing the stirring.

Phélice fixes on the gleaming green-and-white-tiled kitchen; her mémère's
tea-towels folded just so over the stove-door handle, her apron, the long
brown one for over-top good outfits, hangs beside the stove; the two shorter
ones for everyday now worn by Clémence and Léonie, a flowered pink and
a gingham yellow. Léonie joins Clémence, already busy around the stove.
Aurore and Diane automatically go to the right drawers and cupboards,
begin taking out the necessary kitchen ware.

Phélice stands with her arms around herself and marvels at how much
her kitchen is set up just like this. She wryly supposes, that all of their
kitchens hang cups, except the good ones, of course; they are stacked carefully in the back somewhere or set on display in a china cabinet. Cutlery
to the left of the sink, spoons in a jam jar on the table, honey, sugar, and
powdered creamer in the lazy-Susan, also left on the table. Plates and
saucers, together on a top shelf beside the everyday bowls for cereal.
Bigger bowls lower down, nesting one inside the other, pots and pans

stacked to save room, either below in the broiler section of the stove or to the left of the stove. Frying pan with its perpetual sheen of bacon fat either left on the stove or in the stove.

—Mom? she asks, eyes closed to test her theory, —where would Mémère keep her pepper?

She pictures the white-and-green salt and pepper shakers, the everyday set, on the shelf above the stove.

—What do you need pepper for? asks Léonie, turning to her daughter with a preoccupied look on her face.

—I don't need pepper, I am just trying to see if I can guess where the pepper is, explains Phélice.

Léonie looks at her and frowns. She shakes her head and says briskly, —Take this in there, she holds out a pitcher of warm chokecherry sauce for the pound cake.

—But Mom, imagine this . . . all our kitchens are the same! We put our stuff in the same drawers and here . . . she walks over to the small side cupboard beside the back door, —we keep the broom and dustpan in here, and the cookie sheets, she flings open another door, —here! And coffee and tea canisters here, and there's always a stash of candy right about . . . she reaches behind the canisters, —here! she cries delightedly, pulling out a small tin of humbugs.

—Phélice! What has gotten into you? scolds her mother. —Put that back, what's wrong with you?

—Nothing is wrong, Mom. Stuff is just starting to make more sense now. We probably do a lot of things that are the same, all of us, I bet. Like, do you put on both socks and then your shoes? Or do you do sock, shoe, sock, shoe?

Clémence laughs at Phélice. —The state you're in, I'm surprised you could even *find* your socks this morning. Although now that you mention it, I wear these damned pantihose so I guess I'd have to put both legs on first before I . . .

—Don't encourage her Clémence! I don't know where you come up with this stuff, Phélice! Now, please, the food? Léonie gestures once more with the pitcher.

—Think about it, Mom, we inherit our little kitchen habits, she says, popping a humbug in her mouth, —the way we speak, the way we walk, the way we all wear the heels of our shoes down first, she gestures to the shelf of shoes next to the door, —all that says we are . . .

—Hungry, finishes Léonie. Now, come on Phélice, help or get out of the way.

Phelice grins and takes the plate of food from her mother. —I was going to say we are family, Mom, we are *la famille,* whether we like it or not.

Laughing, she goes off into the living room to deliver the sauce.

Clémence looks at Léonie. —You know, she says, —that girl is smart. She does the same things we do, but she watches more and she figures out why we do it. I guess that's what school does to you, einh? Makes you smart.

Léonie smiles apologetically at Clémence, Aurore, and Diane. —Oh, I don't know if she's so smart, smart-ass, maybe, yes, but smart? That's a life thing. That's for us old married ladies, you and me, einh?

Diane goes back to the cupboard for a serving plate. —Well, I heard she was married there for a while anyway. Guess that makes her smart, like us . . . she murmurs.

Aurore lightly touches Diane's shoulder.

When the food is spread out to Léonie's satisfaction, people line up politely and eat themselves into a stupor. Balancing hot cups and plates of chicken, ham, potatoes, and three different kinds of salad—macaroni, jellied and three-bean—they sit and talk and eat some more and drink down to the grounds of Marie's percolator.

Finally satiated, the mourning crowd goes home and only the family remains.

Patrique, Léo, Diane's husband Paul, Clémence's husband Robert, and

Marie's Joseph loosen their ties and belts, stretch out on the couch and reclining La-Z-Boy chairs, intent on a small cat nap to pass the afternoon.

The women ease out of their pointy church shoes, fluff out their stiffened hair-dos, and wander from the living room to the kitchen boxing up left-overs, dividing up desserts.

The last of the dishes are put away. It is time for the catching up, time to talk. Not the polite society talking they've done all morning, but to talk of things Phélice was referring to earlier in the kitchen, the things that make them a family. They will deal with the little bits of jewellery Philia had later. They will fight about the furniture and the house later.

Now they get out the photo albums, they never travel without photo-albums. Phélice adds the two books she has to the table.

Madelaine pulls the books towards her. —Well, I'll be darned. Rubis's book and Philia's too? Where did you get these? she eyes Phélice suspiciously.

—Mémère gave them to me, a couple of years ago, Phélice struggles under her aunt's scrutiny. —I have been looking through them the last little while. They are interesting examples of pioneer life and early medicine, she finishes in her intellectual voice.

—Is that what you think? smirks Madelaine. —Interesting examples of pioneer life? she shakes her head. —Have you had any good dreams lately, Phélice? Seen any spiders around?

—Madelaine, wouldn't you be more comfortable over here? asks Diane. —You could put your feet up, there's a nice little ottoman right here . . .

—What do you mean, have I seen any spiders? Phélice leans closer to Madelaine.

—Oh, nothing. Just that, well, sometimes ghosts come back as spiders and . . .

Clémence laughs out loud, —Oh come off it, Madelaine! Why are you scar-ing the girl with stories like that? And anyway, Philia hasn't had the time to turn in her grave, let alone turn into a spider for Pete's sake!

—But Rubis has, murmurs Aurore to Léonie in the kitchen. Léonie looks at her anxiously.

—What did you say? she hisses.

—Rubis is a spider and Reuville is a fly, sometimes . . . sometimes just a noise, a squeak or a moan in the floorboards, sometimes a candle will go out for no reason, or sputter . . . that's ghosts going by, explains Aurore softly. —I know. I have seen them.

—Don't be crazy. Léonie shakes Aurore's arm a little, as if to wake her. —Don't say things like that. Just a bunch of nonsense and superstition. Stuff Philia tried to fill Phélice's head with and stuff I've been trying to clean out for the last twenty years.

—Philia wasn't wrong, Léonie, Aurore says, her eyes twinkling. —Philia wasn't wrong very often at all, was she? She pats Léonie's hand and walks into the living room, singing softly.

> Au clair de la lune,
> Mon ami Pierrot,
> Prete moi ta plume,
> Pour écrire un mot;
> Ma chandelle est morte,
> Je n'ai plus de feu;
> Ouvre moi ta porte pour l'amour de Dieu.

> Au clair de la lune,
> Pierrot repondit:
> Je n'ai pas de plume,
> Je suis dans mon lit.
> Va chez la voisine:
> Je crois qu'elle y est,
> Car dans sa cuisine
> On bat le briquet.
> Fais do-do mon beau petit frère.
> Fais do-do, tu auras du gâteau.

Maman est en bas, qui fait du chocolat.

Papa est en haut, il boit de l'eau . . .

Léonie follows warily, knowing that when Aurore's eyes get bright like this she is going to talk her crazy talk and nothing will stop her.

–Philia died at night. Bet she hated that, einh? Madelaine grins at Léonie, who is bringing her crotchet bag over to the table.

–She hated nights, was scared of the dark near the end, replies Léonie, not looking at Madelaine.

–Scared of nights? Only nights? I am scared of lots more than that, laughs Clémence. –Sickness and bad things don't only happen at night! People get sick, get hurt, even die during the day. My boy died during the day. Coughed blood all night long. He died at five o'clock in the morning. I prayed to keep the day from coming.

She hesitates. –First time it didn't work to pray.

–Ah! You haven't lived long enough, says Madelaine roughly, looking up at Phélice. –You'll see. Prayers can bounce off of some people like water in a hot pan. Some don't want to get better.

She flips through her battered photo album, stopping at a picture of a plump woman standing next to a very tall, handsome man with a pencil-thin moustache. They are on the porch of her old house in Talon.

[　]　Hélène Touseigne.

Her husband brought her from Winnipeg. She was pale, a doughy thing with big, green-brown eyes that blinked real slow when her husband talked. He was a big shot at the bank of Hotchelaga, in Red River, Manitoba, there.

She was crippled in the arm. It was pitiful really, not more than twenty and not able to use her arm. Got it broke the day before her wedding, apparently, hanging paper flowers for the breakfast they were going to have after and fell off the ladder, right into the big rosebush. She must have landed wrong, and landed hard.

They didn't do such a good job putting the shoulder back in, just bound it up and hoped it would go back in on its own, I guess. The arm was busted in two places. Must of hurt like hell, they were bad breaks. No one could touch her, einh? She'd just mewl like a baby cat. They had her on the morphia.

—But one year is enough, he says.

She blinks.

—We've had Hélène's younger sister over at the house since the accident, helping out with all the work, he finishes quickly, with a little wink.

I think, is that a businessman wink? Or another kind of wink?

She blinks.

—It is not too bad, einh? he tugs at his suspenders. —But I can't have Chérie here in pain all the time.

I go to her, feel through the dress to where the shoulder is hot. Not bad but stuck good. A year!

I pause, wait for the smooth give of bone on bone, felt the strength of scar muscles and the cracks in her cartilage, then the give. I pull quick and hard.

She mews in surprise then starts the scream that's waited a year to come out. Ben is there pushing me away from her.

—What are you doing? Enough! Stop! Now, stop! You've hurt her. Oh Chérie! Oh Hélène! She won't hurt you anymore, bébé! Stop crying Hélène, oh Chérie, it's okay, it's okay.

Hélène is moaning and humped over herself.

I know it can hurt when you fix it after so long. I know I'd have to break her arm to reset that. I know the shoulder will take a few weeks to feel normal again. I know she'll feel better, but she won't tell him.

—If you can, Touseigne, keep some cold-water cloths on her shoulder for the next little while, one hour on, one hour off again, for a day or two. It keeps the swelling down and mix up some of this, I go to the cupboard for a bag of plantain, –in a poultice with egg whites three times a day. Don't wrap it too tight, it'll be tender. As for the arm . . .

She looks at me through her moaning. She doesn't blink.

–I can't do anything. It wasn't set properly in the first place and the break's healed too bad.

–But they said you could fix anyone! he says, puffing himself up to look angry.

He takes his eyes off me and they light on the head of the girl he's deflowered. They linger on the syringe on the kitchen table. He is seeing Hélène's young sister waiting at home in Red River.

–God works the miracle. I don't, I say, putting an end to their silliness. I wonder why some people don't want to be healed. *Qu'elle devient maître de sa misère.* It's something I saw in Philia's book once. I know now what she meant.

She blinks, bows her head, and says softly, –She did her job, Ben, I was just surprised, that's all. We can tell your maman it was worth the trip. Really, I'm sorry I screamed. I was just surprised, that's all. It's all right now, she finishes with a sigh and straightens up.

–It's decided then, I say.

They collect their things and leave. I sit in my rocking chair and begin the prayers for her recovery. I choose the long one. I am very sad, but I choose the long one, some for her, some for me. Clémence can start supper tonight.

–I started supper every night, scoffs Clémence good-naturedly.

Diane slowly turns the pages of Philia's book, looking.

—What are you looking for, ma tante? Maybe I can help, I must have looked through that book a hundred times, says Phélice.

Diane props her elbows on the table, folding her hands under her chin. She confides, —Phélice, have you ever made stock from bones? Let's say the kids are sick, she looks away a little flustered, remembering why Phélice does not have children. —Or if you're in the kitchen anyway, she continues quickly to hide her embarrassment, —ironing, sewing, and all that, boil bones. It's in getting them to boil and not spill over. That's the secret— patience. You get them going for at least four to five hours, to get all the marrow out. You'll get a good rich broth from two big neck bones or, say, the carcass of two chickens.

Never boil onions with the bones. You want to boil onions, boil onions. You want to boil bones, boil bones. Add onions later. Fill the place with that lovely onion and butter smell. Cook 'em 'til you can see through the onions.

But don't boil onions with the bones. Some things, she flutters her hands towards the photo albums and books, —some things just don't cook well together. Like, some of this stuff you know? It might have worked a long time ago, but now? I don't know, she says, shaking her head, laughing stiffly, —I just don't know if you should follow the recipes here.

Phélice lights a cigarette and nods, —I think I know what you mean, some of the ingredients are pretty wild!

She open Philia's scrapbook and begins to read:

> *Annie's boneless pork feet*
>
> *6 pork feet*
> *2 qt. cold water*
> *salt*
> *1 large carrot*
> *1 onion*
> *3 tbsp. pepper*
>
> *Cover pork feet with water, add carrot, onion, celery, and spices, simmer gently*
> *for about 3½ hours or until tender enough to slip bones out easily. Drain,*
> *slip out bones, and press into shape with hands. Place between two platters*

with a weight on top—the big iron works well—let cool overnight. Separate,
dip in melted butter, roll in fine breadcrumbs. Let stand in the refrigerator
after patting well. Pan-broil on lightly greased skillet to a golden brown,
turning frequently.

Garnish with parsley, although radishes cut into roses look nice too.

Bonjour Philia!

Glad to hear that Clémence is back from the camps. She's probably a real big
help around there. Anyway, Donald and I might have a chance to swing up
your way. Can you put us up for a bit? Donald has a bit of the influenza, so we
will wait until he is better to travel. Wouldn't want to infect you and the
babies. I know what that's like.

We are both anxious to see the family—yours and Léo's and Patrique's. Twins,
on both sides? They waited long enough to start having kids and then they go
and have twins. What miracle is that? Tell Blanche and Louise we will bring
the gifts for the baptisms when we get there.

Here is the recipe you wanted. Not sure why some people want to disguise perfectly good feet, but this one lets you do something pretty with the feet that are
damaged in some way.

Be good, your sister, Annie

Madelaine leans over to Phélice and talks over Aurore's head.

—Philia was the one who first noticed Aurore had gifts. She found rabbits
and deer in the kitchen panelling.

Like Philia, Aurore could tell you the colour of music, the smell of colours,
the shape of a taste. Held crying children and the fever broke. She had the
touch to ease all manner of poison from the body, from the blood of
women, to diarrhea of men, poison stuff. It wasn't a gift or a curse you
know, knowing if the unborn was male or female, it was useful.

[   ]   That's a picture of her on the porch of the house in Salmon Arm, before we built the addition.

Sitting on a kitchen chair, just sitting, as if she can hear music, as if she was waiting for someone. When we were kids we were like those forks you use for music tuning, you know? Vibrating, clanking, clicking when they're held against each other. Now, well, now we get along just fine, don't we Aurore?

Aurore starts at the sound of her name. She is so engrossed in Clémence's photo album that she hasn't been following the conversation. She smiles at Madelaine. That's always the best response.

She leans back from the table and points to a picture.

[   ]   Aurore holding a small white and black dog. She is young, smiling and surrounded by children.

She looks at her hands and then places them palm down on the table. —When I touched that little dog I touched the kids through him and I felt their love and their need for him to live. I could hear his heart and his stomach and feel his blood and all his broken bones crunching and sliding every way—in my head I could feel this, you know? Well, then I said a prayer, and my hands got warm and my arms, einh? All the way up my arms. And all I could hear was that dog, his life all through me, and I had my eyes closed and the dog wasn't whining anymore, just still, einh? Then everything was warm, not burning, not tingling—but anyway—then it started to cool and I let the dog go. And he got up and went to the door. I picked up my guitar and started singing this song I wrote for the Mother Marie and the dog came to me and sat at my feet and just listened. When I was done singing, like what? Like a prayer of thanks, I guess, he gets up and goes outside. That's all.

Clémence taps the picture of a wooden building in her photo album.

[   ]   There are two women. Philia and Madame Corneille. Madelaine, Aurore, Diane, Marie, Clémence, and Léonie are the young children gathered around a sign, "La Compagnie Casavant."

—Here is a picture of the clothespin factory where we used to work, she says softly. It was open for a while there, then it closed down . . . it was okay to work there. Even Philia didn't complain. They would cut the rough pieces at the mill, then the boys would sand them in the back there, and the women would put them together with those little rubber tips.

Just inside the door there is a stain. You can't see it in the picture. A whole batch of pins was stained from when Louise, Léo's wife, lost the baby there, standing up. The women kept those bloodied pins and gave them to people as protection against losing a child. The blood of one shed for the sake of others.

You know, I think there could still be some of those pins around. Check the clotheslines around town. Must be pretty faded by now though, I think. Blood fades, she says thoughtfully, gently fingering the ratty paper with a recipe for soap taped beneath the picture of the factory..

Philia's recipe for soap

Should make 8 lbs. of soap
Use beef fat and pork fat mix, 8 cups melted and cleaned
1 10 oz. (small can) of lye (this stuff is in large flakes)
8 cups cold, soft water

Cut a bar into small pieces and melt in some hot water on the stove. Pour into washing machine. What you don't use, add more hot water and keep that in a bottle under the sink for dishes.

This stuff will take the stain out of anything. Especially good for blood. Keep away from delicate things.

Talon 1931

Later that morning I begin to bleed. Philia was right; it hurts, but not a little, a lot! It feels like barbed wire is coming out. The blood is in knots and blobs. One blob is almost as big as my fist! Philia keeps changing the sheets. She gathers up all the bloody sheets and the rags and goes with them.

But she doesn't scold me or yell or anything like Maman would have done. All she says is, —Clémence, you rest now.

Marie comes the first day and looks at me. She clucks and fusses a bit with my blankets and pillow. She and Maman Philia look at each other. Philia nods and Marie presses two matchsticks to the skin over my belly. She says a prayer. Her lips move but there is no sound.

Then Marie sings and hums little songs that sound more like birds singing than the noises of people.

> Une petite chandelle, j'ai allumé ce soir.
> Une petite chandelle pour chasser tout le noir.
> Une petite chandelle pour faire venir l'espoir.
> Une petite chandelle, j'ai allumé ce soir.
> Flamme couleure de miel, ma petite chandelle.
> Lumière pour tout le ciel, chère belle petite chandelle.

She smiles at me and stays for a while, telling me and Léonie stories and feeding us biscuits and tea with honey.

Diane comes too. She rubs my hands between hers and combs out my hair. She traces around my eyes and my mouth. She offers to hold me until I sleep. I haven't been held for a long time. I thought it would feel too funny, but it feels nice.

I sleep and dream of 'Ti Paul and I feel very, very sad. I feel like I am saying goodbye forever and for real. After I wake up I eat toasted bread, with cream and brown sugar this time.

I stop bleeding after three days. I feel better. I had never bled like that in my life! Never like that time and never again. If I live to be a hundred, I can't thank the women enough. I owe them everything.

Robert Casavant leaves his seat in the living room, intrigued by the stories and the pictures. Madelaine smiles at him and shows him a wedding picture.

[   ]   Robert stands behind Clémence, who is seated on a small chair. She wears a pillbox hat with a spray of white lily of the valley caught up in the netting. Her gloved hands hold a rosary. They smile shyly into the camera.

–Is that us? Oh yeah, I think I remember that day . . . Hey Clémence, see this here? Do you remember the day we got married? Ha, ha! Yes, you married me . . . who else would have me? Ha!

He turns to Phélice.

–Clémence and me were married, oh gee, I guess she was about sixteen or thereabouts. Yes, sixteen, and I was probably this side of twenty, for sure. Don't matter how old we were, when I looked at her, I knew she was the one for me. I don't mean angels sang and the heavens parted and all that stuff, gee whiz!

First time I saw her, she was climbing into the back of our truck, and she was pretty ratty-looking under that tarp I can tell you! But next morning I could see she was pretty, all dark hair and blue eyes and strong body. I tell you that woman could have carried me to the church and she nearly did, by jeez! Hey Clémence, remember? How the boys celebrated the night before the wedding? You and your little rosary had some work that day, einh?

What's that, Phélice? Her? Clémence, a healer? Well, ah, now, the power of God takes many forms, you see. It does come through people in the same family, but she wasn't the one that got it in her family.

Clémence, her there, got a faith stubborner than pig thistle! She has this thing with her rosary; you know the hundred prayers and all that? Well, she can pray the devil dizzy, that one, for sure! When she gets on that rosary nothing can make her stop until she's finished. Saw her take sick kids in her arms many a time and pray the sickness right out of them with that faith.

Robert stops talking and scratches himself under the chin. He looks towards the kitchen door, noticing the graceful cobwebs strung from the fluorescent lights to the four corners of the ceiling.

Clémence comes around the table to stand behind her husband, facing those gathered around the table. She puts her hand on Robert's back. Then she removes her little screw-on pearl earrings and drops them in the apron pocket.

When Clémence puts her hand out to touch Robert again, a spark of static electricity snaps between them.

They both jump and Robert laughs, —We still got it, einh Clem? Me and you, ma vieille. You can still shock me, even after all these years!

Clémence looks at him, afraid for a moment that he has read her thoughts, about her dad and the blood she shed because of him. Then she realizes with relief that it's just Robert. Her Robert being kind, being safe. Impulsively, she leans over and kisses his cheek.

The others at the table rib them good-naturedly, making loud smacking noises until Clémence waves her apron at them, shooing them like flies.

[   ]   Madelaine says, —This is a picture of me and my cousin Elisabet, we have our arms around each other, and it looks like we are in love too, einh? But I remember, not an hour before this was taken, I had my hands around her throat!

We were at the farm and all the girls were getting pennies from les mon oncles. One penny for everything that was pretty: hair—a penny; smile—a penny; nice, white teeth—a penny.

Elisabet nearly cleaned them out that day. She was a beautiful girl back then. I was too shy to go up to those big, grown-up boys so I stayed near ma tante Philia. I asked her if she thought I was pretty.

She turned me full around once. Then she put her hand under my chin and said, —Madelaine, some are born pretty, others are born smart. You are lucky, you were born smart.

She got me started peeling potatoes for supper, with a peppermint melting deliciously hot and cool all at the same time in my mouth.

I wanted to ask her if she thought Elisabet was pretty, but I never cared too much for Elisabet anyway.

Later, I caught up with the little sainte Elisabet behind the chicken coop. I told her ma tante Philia had given me a peppermint for her too. Got her to stand there, pretty eyes closed and pretty mouth opened. Dropped a pretty big chicken turd right into that pretty mouth!

Oh, there was hell to pay after that! I had the Evil in me for sure that day!

Philia was right, some are born pretty, some are born smart, laughs Madelaine, shaking her head and wiping the tears of laughter from her eyes with the corner of Clémence's apron.

Marie, still chuckling, turns to another picture. [   ]   Gaston Corneille on crutches. Marie-Ange, his wife, beside him, holding a baby.

She tells Phélice, —Now here was another one like Madelaine, not too pretty, but smart . . . that's the old man Corneille and his wife, "Marie des anges," we used to call her. Gaston'd leave early November for the bush. After clearing what he could for his farm, he left Marie-Ange, and the little ones, to make extra money in the lumber camps. Most men did that back then, to get a little extra money for seed and stock and more land.

Some went to the mine, it was closer to home, but the big money was in the camps. You could make $4.50 for each cord you cut and piled. And if you worked the 108-day minimum, the timber company refunded your train fare, both ways!

It was worth it, if you could stand shaving with an axe, drinking tea from the same tin bowl your stew had been in, never undressing. But I suppose those are women's concerns. As far as that goes, it made the men a little more appreciative of the comforts of home when they got back.

He had been gone about a week or so. Diane and I were with Marie-Ange at her place, getting a start on the Christmas baking, those white cookies with raisins that Gaston and the kids loved so much.

Quick as you can say knife, Diane stopped mixing the batter. She sat down, muttering something about purple chicks and thunder. I was taking a tray of cookies out from the oven, when I heard her say,

—Blood.
There is blood in the snow.

Sky is dark. Bacon coloured clouds.

Man shouting. Mouths making long O's of steam. Gaston is breathing.

Look at him. Steady—nnngh—teeth clenched, eyes shut tight.

Axe? There.

What?

Leg. There.

Now, stop it Marie, stop it.

So I did.

Marie-Ange was so pale she looked like she was going to disappear on us!

–It is finished. He is fine, I said.

She put her head down on the table and began to cry. The baby whimpered at the sound then let out a bellow to remind us that he was there too!

–The baby needs you, Diane said briskly, rising from her chair and scooping up more dough, dividing it carefully.

Marie-Ange raised her hand to Diane, their fingertips touching over the bowl. She looked up at us, raised her eyes to us. –Merci, she whispered.

Don't not need a merci, but it is nice to hear.

Sometimes the blood smells metallic, other times like milk, or like a raw egg a raw wound, something not yet healed.

That blood poured on the grass, the face there is a child unborn.

My fingernail is long, sharp, hard. It pulls through clots, red and dark and small like beans.

Each bean, a heat from inside the body, steaming in the cool morning air, released from its responsibility.

x Rubis

Marie remembers the scent of her own blood—

▧ Talon 1943

Awake and peeking out of the crack of dawn.
Checking the black lumps of clotted night blood.

Reaching for a plate on the top shelf sends a warning to my womb.
Each clothespin I attach clothes with onto the line above my head is a
refusal to be a slave to my body. Each cough is a reminder that I am.

Whisper my Joseph's name-

—It has been a while . . . could you hold me?

But he doesn't want me to start bleeding again

—It's too soon. You just lost the baby.

Put raw egg on my face and in my hair for shine.
Watch my hands cut tomatoes, cupping the orb, slicing it.
A sharp knife is a thing of beauty.

This morning it is one month since Reuville was stopped.

Hear someone laughing.
Check for coyotes along the treeline.
Check for magpies.

Marie speaks to Phélice as she helps herself to more salted peanuts from
the crystal bowl at her left.

—Oh! These peanuts are straight salt. Here, try some. You know, I think salt
has a better song than sugar.

We have so much salt in us
blood
tears

we hear salt better.

When you bleed, you cry.
When you cry, it's like bleeding
from the face.
The two salts hear each other,
and when one is being released
the other one shows up to keep it company,
like the music of a song can haunt you until you remember the words.

Remember this Raoul

The old songs, the songs that heal
are kept deep
within the place where blood comes from.

Some people can't hear the songs,
just like some can't hear the sound of the ocean in a big seashell
and others see nothing in their teacup but loose leaves.

Some look at their children—see a body, a face, maybe some hair—
while others see everything that has been and everything that will be
for that child.

I love you Raoul. I see the world welcoming you. You will be safe.

x Rubis

Aurore waves a fly away from the pound cake. She leans over towards Phélice and tenderly tucks a stray strand of hair behind her ear.

She smiles and says softly, —Philia told me this story about why we have that little divot under our noses. She said, "Before you were born, God took you in His arms and whispered to you all the secrets of the world, all the miracles, and everything that would happen to you. Then He put His finger upon your lips and said, "Shhh!" So that little indent is actually God's fingerprint. I believe that. You already know everything. Believe that, she says, patting Phélice's hand.

Marie adds, —That's right, every child is marked by God, and accounted for.

Léonie looks up sharply from her crocheting. —Some babies are lost, she says, yanking on the wool. —Just lost. I wish you could remember at least that, Aurore.

—I know where mine are, Léonie, Aurore murmurs. —Do you remember yours?

Phélice opens her mouth to speak, but Diane comes in from the kitchen and offers, —Tart, anyone?

Marie chokes until tears come into her eyes. Everyone at the table stares at her. Diane quickly puts the tray of tarts down. She solicitously rubs Marie's back, whispering furiously into her good ear.

Marie comes to herself and waves Diane away. —I didn't mean anything. I didn't mean you! No, I didn't say anything about that, I didn't . . . all right?, All right! she shouts. Diane's backrubbing has become almost rough. —Enough! That's enough, I . . . I am all right now.

She edges forward on her chair, away from Diane. —Diane, really, I wasn't laughing about you being a tart. Just a bit of peanut went down the wrong tube, is all, she says weakly.

Madelaine rises from the table and puts her hand on Aurore's arm. She nods towards the livingroom and Aurore picks up the plate of tarts.

Before leaving to serve the men, Madelaine pours a cup of tea for Marie. —Here, drink this Marie. You shouldn't talk while you eat. Maybe don't talk so much, einh?

She pats her cousin's shoulder, picks up the tea pot, and goes to the living room.

Phélice smiles. —Does this family have a habit of losing babies? Do we put them down and walk away or something?

Léonie glares at Diane, —Ask the tart.

—Mom, whoa! Why would you call ma tante a tart? Was she the wicked one in her younger days? laughs Phélice, reaching for her cigarettes.

Diane looks up.

▓ Talon 1929

—Have you completely lost your mind? screams Philia. Have you no decency? No shame? No pride? What in the world were you thinking, Diane? This is absolutely impossible! No, this cannot be allowed! I will not allow this!

Diane rests her head on her arms on the table. She sighs. Marie puts her hands on Diane's arm and clucks sympathetically.

—And you! says Philia, rounding on Marie, I suppose you knew all along about this? Of all the people in the world, you are supposed to protect your sister! Your poor mother would die of shame if she knew this! Absolutely unforgivable! Your mother is crying from the gates of Heaven, wondering why she can't get in, and it is because of this slut of a daughter! Do you know that, Diane? Do you? You are keeping your sainted mother from her heaven because you can't keep your drawers up. Mother of God! And with Roland Trefflé of all pigs at the trough. If I had known what was in store for that boy I would have rung his neck the day he was born. And you too! I should have killed you when I had the chance.

Diane lifts her head. Tears streak her face; she raises a hand towards Philia.

—Non, ma tante Philia, please, non. Don't say that. Please, not that. I, I am so sorry, I didn't know. I am so . . .

Philia rears for another attack.

—You didn't know if a man puts his thing inside you, you would become pregnant? You didn't know that? You, who watches animals day in and day out, you didn't know that? On top of being a slut, you are a liar now too, is that it? Is it? Tell me! Answer me, girl!

Diane moans and drops her head back on her arms.

Philia reaches over and yanks her braid, hard. Diane howls. She struggles to turn and face Philia.

Philia's tone is deadly calm and hard. —Look at me, girl. Look me in the eyes, like you did when you were fucking that mongrel. Look at me when I'm talking to you.

Philia gives the braid a mighty shake and Diane is almost pulled out of her chair.

—Ma tante Philia! Marie jumps up from her chair and tries to wrench Philia's hand from Diane's hair.

—Come on! Enough! Enough! Let her go! Let my sister go!

—What will we do? Philia says, in a dead voice. —What will we do? How can we fix this? How? She punctuates each question with a small yanks on Diane's braid.

She suddenly drops the braid as if it were a snake that has bitten her. She looks at Marie, who stares right back at her. Philia looks at her hand. It is cold, a searing cold like touching frozen metal, but there are no marks. Marie drops her gaze.

Philia eyes Diane's sobbing figure.

—Oh stop your blubbering, you. It was only a shake. Maybe that will wake you up, make you understand your responsibilities now. Let me think . . .

Philia folds herself into a chair, deflated.

—Ma tante Philia . . . whispers Marie.

—Shut up you! I'm trying to think.

—But ma tante, I . . .

—Shut up Marie, Philia says more softly. She rubs her eyes, rests her forehead on her hands.

The kitchen is quiet except for the ticking of the clock and Diane's sniffling. A dog barks outside. All three look at the back door, then at each other. Philia rises, almost painfully, from her chair and places her hands flat on the table.

—Blow your nose, Diane, and you, she points her chin at Marie, —you take her home. Delphis is back. We'll talk about this tomorrow.

Marie offers her handkerchief to her sister. Diane stifles a sob, blows her nose, and bites her own hand to keep from crying again. Marie holds her up as they walk to the front door.

—You won't tell mon oncle Delphis about this will you? asks Marie, her hand on the doorknob.

—It is really none of your affair what I discuss with my husband, Philia says firmly. —We will have to decide this thing between all of us.

—Please don't tell Papa about this, whispers Diane. Please, ma tante! I will do whatever you say, I . . .

A child begins to cry in an upstairs bedroom.

—Now you've woken Léonie. Well, thank you very much for a lovely visit, girls. Go away until tomorrow, sighs Philia, mounting the stairs to get her daughter.

The two girls hesitate just inside the door. Diane turns around.

—Ma tante Philia?

Philia stiffens, her hand on the banister. —Yes?

—I am sorry, you know.

Philia fixes the girl with a stare that belies her own confusion and desperation. —I know you are, Diane. But this isn't fixed with a sorry. This will take more, much more. But it can be fixed. Leave it to me. Come back tomorrow.

—Ma tante Philia?

—Tomorrow, Philia says, waving her hand behind her back to show she's heard. She just can't talk to her right now.

She calls up the stairs, —J'arrive, Léonie j'arrive. Christly bawling, worse
than a calf!

Phélice and Léonie are looking through Léonie's bag for the special little
silver scythe, a gift from her pépère Raoul, that she uses to cut lengths of
thread. Madelaine and Aurore are deep in conversation with Robert and
Clémence about the wild crocuses and lily of the valley they found in their
back yard the other day.

Marie looks towards the window and nonchalantly moves Philia's scrapbook
so that it is in front of Diane. Diane places her hand on the collection of
recipes and letters. Closing her eyes, she carefully slips two letters out.

Ma chère Philia,

*Your package has arrived, safe and sound, if a little shaky from the long trip.
She will be all right, in about five months I think.*

*Already she is hard at work with the house things. Her maman would be proud
of the way she is pitching in. There are no distractions here, except for the
hired help, who will be gone in a few weeks anyway, so don't worry. She is a
good girl, in spite of it all.*

*She even made us some pea soup the other day. We didn't have any ham handy,
so she used chicken instead. Pretty good all the same.*

*I will see to it that she writes to that Paul fellow. Not right now, of course, but
soon. If you're sure that's what you want.*

*Well, that's all for now. We are all healthy and doing well. Pretty busy with this
new batch of horses. Everyone sends a big hello your way.*

Be good. Your sister, Annie.

Ma chère Philia,

That was just a pity that Blanche lost another baby. She must have taken it pretty hard. I know how she gets. Remember when the bad luck found her here? Tell her we will all be praying for her. Tell Patrique to lay off for a while.

Diane is doing fine. Her bundle is off with the de Champlains, they are good people. Pierre, that's what they baptized him, will be well taken care of.

Diane wants to go home, figures she and this Paul Poisseau have some business now. Let me know if you want her back.

Have already promised the grizzly hide to the neighbour, but I will see about getting some back if you have your heart set on it. If you are making something big I will dig up my pattern for the Hudson Bay blanket coat. Use the big needle.

And remember, leftovers can still make a pretty fine thing.

> *Be good. Your sister, Annie.*

Marie watches her sister go to the kitchen. Phélice pushes her chair back. —I'll go see if ma tante Diane needs any help, she says, standing and stretching.

—No! Wait, says Marie, sliding a photo album in front of Phélice and flipping it to the picture of a young Marie standing beside her father Léo.

—I don't know how it all works exactly, Phélice, she says, casting an anxious eye towards the kitchen door. —I just know it felt like a shiver. All the hairs on my arms would stand on end. Sometimes, when there was a lot of water, like at Brisson's one time, it even made the hairs all over my legs stand up! But mostly it was in the arms.

Marie catches the smell of celery. No wait, pennies, she can smell warm pennies! Just like when she was going towards water . . .

Marie says, —Some people took a médaille, you know from the church, with Marie on it. Non, non, not me, she laughs, —The Other One, La Vièrge Marie. They would pray and fling the médaille. Where it landed was supposed to be water. I didn't do that. Seems a bit much to ask from a piece of metal, don't you think? A bit too iffy for me, she chuckles.

Phélice rubs Marie's arm, laughing. She picks up the smell something. Is that celery? She has forgotten all about going to help Diane. Leafing through the scrapbook, she finds a loose piece of lined paper. It is a poem. Squinting over the name at the bottom, Phélice is sure it says "Diane Morin."

Diane comes back to the table, wrinkling her nose, catching the smell of something. Marie notices Diane is a bit pale, but smiling, so she says nothing.

Phélice asks Diane to read the poem. Diane blushes and declines. A little coaxing is in order, and a small drop of chokecherry wine is poured to grease her voice.

Diane pushes up her glasses, licks her lips, and reads. She remembers when she wrote the poem, just after the accident in the mine. Her voice rings out, as strong and sharp and clear as the blow of an axe.

Nous ne parlons plus en roche percée

Let us say this now,
this is for everyone who speaks our name
as a mouthful of hot spiders,
for everyone who told us to go home,
if we dare slather our language between loaves of laughter.

We remember
that for every inch that some find us useful,
there is a mile of wide prejudice.

We do not speak the rock of Gaspé or the sibilant waters of the Saint Laurent.
We do not speak the cliffs and the shores of salt any longer.

We imbibed sky and wind, earth, animals and woods of here.

We are from here.

We are here, this is us.

We are the French-Canada
that lives as jewels in the earth.
We are the French-Canada
that fashions medals to protect the maimed of this earth.

Diane Morin

les femmes de Talon

J'entends le moulin

tique, tique, taque.
J'entends le moulin
taque.

Mon père a fait bâtir maison,
l'a fait bâtir à trois pignons
tique, tique, tique, taque
tique, tique, taque.

So sings Rubis softly, as she begins to unbraid her hair.

No one speaks until Diane takes another sip of chokecherry wine. Two of them catch each other's eyes, in warning.

Marie's husband, Joseph, walks softly from the darkened living room. He limps up to the table, bleary eyed. —Jewels in the earth, medals for the maimed, he mutters. —Very good there, Diane, very good. He comes up behind Phélice and places his hands on the back of her chair.

—Phélice, don't ever work in a mine, he rasps. —It'll kill you fast, or it'll kill you slow, he raps on his wooden leg, —but it will surely kill you.

—What happened in the mine, mon oncle? asks Phélice quietly, not turning around. Her mon oncle Joe so rarely speaks she is afraid of startling him.

Joseph grunts and shuffles heavily into the kitchen.

Robert clears his throat. —The mine was a place where men went to work, to make extra money. We all did, even your dad, Phélice.

Léonie shoots him a warning look.

He sighs, oblivious to Léonie's narrowed eyes and pinched mouth. —It was tough though. We were used to making things grow, seeing green and sun and smelling animals, then suddenly—wham! Nothing in front of you but a seam of black coal. The dead smell that furnaces eat. Jewels? he chuckles grimly, —That's what we were digging for all right and some of us became jewels too, so long underground!

The women guffaw at that one.

—You know, he continues thoughtfully, caught up in the memory, —people in trouble don't scream as loud as they think they do . . . When Joe, he nods quietly towards the kitchen, —started making little woofs, we didn't stop right off. Then the real screaming started and we dropped the picks and shovels and buckets and got the hell over to him. Reuville was standing over him.

⌧ Talon 1941

We were trying to figure out a way to lift the bugger up without having him come apart. He was wedged between two cars and with all the grease and the blood and the dark, it was hard to tell where he stopped and the metal started. Couldn't even see the whites of his eyes, his face was screwed up so tight.

By the time we got him out of there we had a tourniquet on, but we couldn't find the rest of his leg. Marie was there, her and Joe weren't married yet, so that's good. And Madelaine was there. The blood-and-bone ladies.

Marie looks like she's already somewhere else and she stops the bleeding. Madelaine, as usual, looks mad.

–Diane told us to come. Where is the leg? she says.

–Back there, I say.

She mutters and feels around his body. Marie hunkers down beside her. They look at each other and Madelaine says, –You will need a wagon, do not drag him around anymore. He is out, so he can not feel too much, but no use causing more damage. Bring him to the house.

So, we hitch the team and she helps us haul him up.

Later on, after he is cleaned up and everything, I slip in to see him. Marie's in the kitchen scrubbing, boiling water, and lye soap over everything. I knock real loud so she can hear me. Bang my boots against the doorframe.

–Is he awake? I say.

–Non, Madelaine is with him though. We have to watch for fever now. Aurore is coming. Clémence isn't here, she says, intent on her work.

I know it's serious if Marie isn't smiling.

I go to the back room. Madelaine's kneeling by the bed, doing the rosary.

–What did you bring? she asks.

–L'eau bénite, I say.

This gets her attention. She looks up.

–From the church?

I pull the flask of whiskey from my jacket. She gets up and takes the bottle from me.

—Yours?

—Non, got some from Reuville.

She lifts the flask to her lips, fills her mouth, swallows, fills her mouth again, and swallows. I nod, take the bottle and throw back a shot myself, just to keep her company.

—He's okay then? I ask.

—Will be, probably. He is too old to farm and should never have been in the mine in the first place. L'Abbé is looking for a new bédeau. Maybe he can do that. And mon oncle Léo needs help at the shoe shop. A guy with one leg is not going to steal any shoes, einh?

—He lose the leg then?

She looks at me, the way she can, like she sees you in your underwear or worse.

—You lost the leg, shithead! she laughs.

She keeps laughing and nudges me in the ribs until I laugh too.

Marie blows her nose loud in the kitchen. We hear Aurore come in, and quickly kneel down to finish the rosary.

—Aaah, what a mess, einh? I say.

—It will be fine, she says, as if it has already been decided.

Madelaine sips her wine and spits pieces of cork into her hand, muttering darkly, —I do not snarl.

—Mon oncle Robert, Phélice sneaks a look at her mother, —what was my dad like?

Aurore rubs her eyes. Marie self-consciously smoothes her hair. Diane looks into the bottom of her teacup and is startled by the images in the leaves. There are faces in my tea, she thinks. A piece of rope, a curled baby under a crescent moon, the barrel of a gun. Now? Surely not now. Not these signs, no, not again. She has seen these before, just before . . .

Hearing my name in the thunder.
Name drowned
Someone calling through thunder

While I sleep
Reuville sits
suspenders on a bony frame
hands clasped, nesting in his lap.

My sister Marie lays
head near his legs.
Her eyes glow with his presence.
He goes in there
inside her
and I can tell
he is not smiling.

Diane swats irritably at a fly and nervously clears her throat. She looks Léonie, still smarting from the lost baby remark. She looks into her cup, the signs are still there, and Philia, Philia is not. Looking at Phélice, she says, —I'll tell you about your father, Phélice. You see, in heaven they dine on decisions. In hell, they gorge on doubts. In Talon there was always plenty to keep both sides fat. A few people catering to heaven, a few feeding hell. Everyone adding a little something, everyone. And after a big feed there are always dirty dishes, einh?

Phélice nods, uncertain where this is going. Léonie leans forward, ready to stop Diane at any moment.

—And your dad was like that, a dirty dish. Reuville Trefflé was sour and mean and had the Evil in him as deep as a whiskey barrel. He was beautiful though. All of us thought so. All that curly black hair and deep brown eyes! He was tall and graceful, like a big cat. Skin always shiny, oily, like he had just eaten pork.

Diane stops and sips from her glass of wine. —His brother, Roland, was beautiful too, she says quietly. —But all those Trefflés had rags in the head when it came to the bottle. And having grown up with Baptiste beating them at every turn, well, you become what you are taught, she says firmly, daring the others to contradict her.

—Reuville was a bad one, all right, Philia was right about him all along, nothing but a hoodlum! Aurore pronounces, getting a grateful nod from Léonie.

—There's something else we have to tell you Phélice, Diane says, handing Marie her cup to look into.

Marie stares back at her and passes the cup on to Aurore.

Léonie looks down, digs in her bag for her crocheting things and announces that she must go home to get her special hook. Marie restrains her with a little shake of her head. Léonie looks close to tears but sits back down.

Everyone becomes very quiet. There is some shifting in chairs. Diane clears her throat. The men look up at their wives. The women lower their eyes. In silence, they agree. This is best left to the women.

Robert leaves the table to wake Patrique and Paul, still asleep on the living room. Joseph thumps past them and shakes Léo.

—Come on, vieux bonhomme, let's show them the truck.

They find their hats and coats and leave the house, the screen door slapping shut behind them.

The women draw closer. Madelaine grunts and rises. She gets the bottle of Five-Star and the shot glass from the cupboard under the sink, behind the potato bucket. She pours her own drink into Diane's teacup, to swirl away the images left by the leaves.

‒Medicine.

She underscores the meaning by slowly pouring only one ounce for each in turn. Each woman drinks her share with the solemnity of communion.

Phélice looks expectantly at each of them in turn.

‒Here is a picture of Pierre de Champlain, says Diane.

[   ]   A couple stand in front of a sign that says "Winnipeg, Manitoba." The woman holds a baby so it will face the camera. "1929" is scrawled on the back of the photo.

Phélice looks uncertainly at the photo, not sure what this has to do with her father. She senses that she is finally getting what she asked for. She looks more intently at the picture. ‒You would think that there were more names in the world to choose from, einh?

The women stare at her.

‒I mean, you know, my husband's name was Pierre de Champlain. Good thing I didn't stay married to him, einh? There would have been some mess around Christmas time.

Phélice is talking to herself. Clémence plays with Léonie's yarn. Léonie pinches the bridge of her nose as though her glasses are hurting her. Aurore takes Madelaine's hand. Marie and Diane lean towards each other, eyes closed.

Marie's mouth trembles. She opens her eyes and raises her head to speak, but Diane lays a hand on her arm.

‒Non, merci ma belle, she says softly into her good ear, ‒I will say this.

▨ Talon 1929

‒So, what are we going to do then, Philia? Just ship her off to Annie's and that's that? What's Léo going to say about this? drawls Delphis. He stuffs tobacco into his pipe and searches his pockets for a match.

—It will be better for everyone if she goes away for a while, and Annie certainly could use the help. Léo will do whatever I think is best for those girls. You know that. He's gotten a little soft in the head since Louise passed on. Diane reminds him too much of her, he's said as much to me. Having just Marie to worry about will be a help to him.

She lowers her voice until it is almost menacing, —We have to be careful about this, Delphis, otherwise there is no hope for a good marriage between Diane and Paul Poisseau.

—Does she want to marry Paul?

—She thinks she wants to marry Roland Trefflé! Can you imagine? Of course, that will never happen, huffs Philia.

—Is he already gone?

—Yes, to British Colombia. Left last night. And he will never hurt anyone like he's hurt Diane, not ever again, says Philia, her eyes narrowing, her fingers tracing the patterns of flowers on the faded oilcloth.

Delphis looks up sharply. —What? Philia, what do you mean by that?

—What do you think I mean? I am protecting my family, and every other young vièrge that bastard ever lusts after.

—Now Philia, this is not right. You don't want to get mixed up in anything like that. You know you can't just . . .

—I can. And I did.

—What did you do to him? Delphis raises his hands in surrender. —Non, non, don't tell me. I don't want to know.

Philia's eyes darken. She rearranges the sugar bowl and the jar of spoons between them.

—Anyways, it's not going to kill him, she says to placate him.

—I don't want to know, Delphis says firmly, his voice rising, smoke wreathing his head.

–Fine, I won't tell you then.

–Fine, he puts his pipe down on the ashtray. –I'm going to bed.

–I'll just tidy up a bit, Philia murmurs.

–You might want to tidy up *before* you make a mess, Philia. Delphis
squeezes her shoulder on his way out of the kitchen.

Philia takes the pipe from the ashtray, carefully cleans it out, adds her own
tobacco she has hidden in the linen drawer, and enjoys a quiet smoke in the
kitchen.

Things could get a little quiet for Monsieur Roland Trefflé, she thinks.
What's a pig when he can't make more pigs? If his oinker doesn't work? He
becomes bacon, and we eat him. She smiles grimly.

–Phélice, Pierre was my son, Diane says firmly, ignoring a sour smell waft-
ing around her. –I gave him to the de Champlains after he was born,
because, because . . . her voice cracks, –because I couldn't keep him.

–It was Annie, Philia's sister in Montana, who took care of me and she
found a family for him. It was the de Champlains who named him Pierre. I
didn't get to name him or anything, they took him the day he was born.
Annie took pity on me and told me what he was baptized, after they took
him to Winnipeg.

–Pierre's father was . . . she hesitates and looks over at Marie, who nods
encouragingly. –gone, and I was too young to keep him and no one knew
but Annie and Marie and Philia, of course. It wasn't something we talked
about back then. It was a sin really, a sin, unmentionable. But now that
Philia is gone I can say this aloud. We . . .

Phélice holds up her hand for Diane to stop. She looks for a long time at
the picture.

–Why tell me now? she asks softly, still looking at the picture.

—Well, Diane begins hesitantly, all the while rolling and unrolling the napkin in front of her, then flapping it out to waft away the sour smell. —I thought you should know why you would be so attracted to him, him being so much like Reuville, your dad. Ah . . . well, different than you, and all. And why you couldn't have children . . .

—What? Like my dad? How? says Phélice shaking her head.

She too can smell something like milk, soured milk. It makes her restless and angry, like in her dream with the unknown man in pain. The man who is freezing, his bones breaking —What are you talking about? And what do you mean, why we couldn't have children? How do you know about that? She looks accusingly at her mother.

Léonie refuses to be drawn into this. She looks down at her crocheting.

Diane sighs, —It was Philia. Philia told us about Pierre's temper, him hurting you, hitting you, she says in a hushed whisper. —She did something to Pierre's hands so they couldn't hit you anymore, see? And well, she had done something to Pierre's father so that he couldn't have any more children. Sort of a punishment I suppose, for what happened to me. And well, because of that, Pierre, his son, couldn't have any either. Maybe that's why he was angry all the time, maybe that made him want to hurt you. So you see, it wasn't your fault that you couldn't have babies. It was all because of Philia . . .

—Do not blame this on Philia, Madelaine scolds, waving her hand as if to clear the air. —Why don't you take responsibility, once and for all, Diane? Your whole life has been a bed of roses because of what Philia did for you. And don't you forget that.

—Forget? Forget? says Diane, her voice righteous with indignation, her eyes brimming. —How could I forget, Madelaine? When did she ever let me forget? When Phélice wrote to say that she and a Monsieur Pierre de Champlain from Winnipeg were getting married, did she let me forget? Non! In her eyes I was a stain, a mistake, and she reminded me every day that the stain was spreading. "Infecting the innocent," she said. Every breath I took, I prayed that Phélice would not marry that boy. I . . .

—Wait, wait, interrupts Phélice. Do you mean to tell me that, she says slowly as though words were a new toy for her mouth, —that you, she is looking at Diane straight in the face, —are my mother-in-law?

Diane hangs her head and nods.

—Jésus, breathes Phélice. She touches the photo in silence. The women shift nervously in their chairs.

Phélice looks up at Diane. —I'm sorry I ended up hating your son, ma tante. He was a bit of a crazy bastard you know? No offence, but I'm *glad* we never had kids!

Diane slowly raises her head. —You aren't angry? she asks incredulously.

—Angry? No, of course not. Listen, like I was telling Mom, this is the sixties. Divorces happen. The marriage didn't work out because, well, you know. The final straw came when I thought I was pregnant. He said that he couldn't be possibly the father because he had had the mumps when he was a teenager, so . . . Phélice trails off, wondering for a wild second if Philia could have caused that. And what about the miscarriage that followed?

The women all look at each other. Smiles pass across their eyes.

She is unaware of the conversation rippling through Diane and Marie.

—Will you tell her who the father was?
—If she asks.
—Diane!
—No. Look, she is so happy right now.
—Finish this.

Diane smiles warmly at Phélice.

Léonie, her head still bowed over her crocheting, says, —Yes, and imagine, Diane could have been your ma tante belle-mère as well if she and Roland Trefflé had married.

Roland's name goes off like a bomb. No one moves in the silence. Phélice's smile breaks, leaving nothing but pale realization in its place. If Roland was her father's brother, she married her first cousin.

Diane's smile remains fixed as she seeks out Marie, questioning her.

—What?!
—It's coming.

—You heard me, Léonie continues briskly. —I wasn't married into that family without hearing a thing or two. Reuville was a bastard, no doubt about that, but he never ran off, like Roland did to you, Diane. Reuville stayed. Probably just too drunk to find the road. But don't make yours sound like the Immaculate Conception, Madame Poisseau. We are all human. We all make mistakes. We all have had to live with the consequences of our actions. That's how we've survived for so long. We are smart, aren't we? Aren't we? she asks determinedly, finally looking each of the women in turn.

—We are smart. And we take care of each other, says Madelaine, placing her arms on the table and leaning forward. —Isn't that right Clémence?

—Yes, concedes Clémence, nodding. —Yes, we take care of each other. I couldn't have made it without you, she says simply. —You all know that.

Phélice's mouth opens and closes like a fish out of water. Her mother slides a package of cigarettes in front of her. Clémence strikes a match and holds it up to Phélice. Phélice takes a cigarette and leans toward the flame, but remains mute.

Léonie frowns and brushes a fly from Phélice's forehead.

Reuville begins to stir inside Phélice. His rage swells her blood, its weight gains rhythm, superimposing her own heartbeat. This new pounding is lulling, hypnotic. One side of her leans anxiously inward, eager to hear more clearly; the other side recoils in horror at the shape she recognizes from her dreams, the man in pain.

no white wings here now no smile
no lady

corner of eye grab throat with hooks rip throat from coyote bitches
howling

am power   fullthecrack
movenow yesgo
nownowhere and here and here nowgoandkill

Diane stares unbelievingly at the menacing glow seeping into Phélice's eyes. Cracks, she thinks, a little crack is spreading inside her with all this. Cracks, like between floorboards . . . like where Reuville lives, for a while, in Marie, in my dream, in this house . . . and now in Phélice.

—When you build a house there shouldn't be cracks in the floor, right Diane? Aurore says anxiously, wary of the presence in Phélice's eyes. She whispers anxiously, —Remember when we built the addition on the house? After Guy died? We made sure there were no cracks anywhere, remember? It's not good to have cracks, right Madelaine?

She turns to Madelaine, who opens her mouth to answer but stops. Her hand flutters to her mouth when Phélice stares at her with dark eyes.

Phélice takes her cigarette with her thumb and first finger and reaches awkwardly towards the black glass ashtray. Her ash hits the table intact, and rolls softly towards Aurore. Phélice exhales slowly and stares, throwing daggers at Aurore and Diane through the smoke.

They know who she is.

—Shut your hole she rasps.

Marie looks up sharply. Her eyebrows arch in surprise. She hears Reuville's voice.

—Léonie? she whispers, never looking away from Phélice.

Léonie blinks slowly, puts down her crochet hook and carefully removes her glasses.

—What? she asks.

Marie nods towards Phélice.

Madelaine purses her lips and thumps her purse onto the table.

Léonie looks over at her daughter. She leans forward then jumps back when Phélice turns her head and stares.

–Phélice? whispers Léonie.

Phélice's blank-face grin turns to a snear. She shakes her head.

Clémence says quietly, –We better get started, before the men come back.

Madelaine purses her lips and thumps her purse onto the table. She fishes for the blue rosary. She kisses the cross then hands it to Clémence, who in turn kisses it and begins her one hundred prayers.

–Je Vous salut Marie, pleine de grâce. Le Seigneur est avec Vous. Vous êtes bénite entre toute les femmes et Jésus le fruit de vos entrailles est bénit. Sainte Marie, Mère de Dieu, priez pour nous pécheurs, maintenant et à l'heure de notre mort. Amen. Je Vous salut Marie . . .

Phélice blinks slowly, trying to focus on all six women at the same time. Her voice is a snail that squeals like a blade being pulled through gravel.

– Go to hell. Allofyous.

–Welcome back, you bastard, Diane says casually, saluting Phélice with her glass.

Colours swarm to life before them. A grainy picture show. Eight people on horseback, Patrique, Léo, and Philia in the lead. Five girls behind them in fan formation.

Diane recognizes herself as the one with streaks of blood where her eyes should be. Totally absorbed by the people in the mist, smiling and talking to them as though it were the most natural thing in the world to converse with ghosts.

Marie sees the child beside Diane. She is the one with no ears, dressed all in blue and carrying water on her shoulders. Her hair ripples and streaks the water red. Marie touches her own ears in Philia's kitchen and smiles.

Aurore is pleased with the image of herself as a winged dragonfly. Her head swivels like an owl, looking for the one who is projecting these images. She cannot know her, but she recognizes Rubis and delightedly sends up a spray of northern lights from her hands.

Léonie wishes she could not see herself, the one right beside Philia. She shrinks at her deformity. It is what people always notice first about her. Then she recognizes the silver scythe in her hand. Her embarrassment turns to shy happiness when she recognizes it as the strength of Raoul's confidence in her. She drinks in Rubis's conviction that a woman will always protect her family. Léonie sits up a little straighter, her face aglow.

Madelaine is the rider with a thunder cloud for a cloak. She snaps the reins of small, highly polished bones, making them shimmer with blue light, like her rosary. Warmth flows over and through her as she joins a voice that begins from everywhere at once and continues forever. She is singing with Rubis.

Images flash for an instant, then dissolve.

Rubis dancing with Raoul.

Baptiste, grunting and grumbling, snags his snowshoe on the wire. He bends over.

Roland picking up a haversack, turning around.

Léonie looking at something on the floor, holding a poker in her hands.

Pierre bent over Phélice's shaking body, his fists still clenched.

Phélice in a dark kitchen, holding a crystal by a length of white thread.

Reuville slumped over. He looks up.

—Go away! shouts Madelaine, rising and slamming both her fists on the table in front of Phélice. —You are dead! Go away, you are not wanted here.

Phélice blinks and says from far away, —Dead? Why?

Diane laughs out loud. Aurore quickly pats her on the back. They must not lose their heads, not now.

Aurore looks calmly at Phélice, —You are not to feel guilty Phélice, ma fille. Pierre and you, how were you to know? No harm done there, she says in a brisk, friendly tone.

A ripple passes over Phélice's face, like wind over water. She says in a strangled voice, —I'm . . . I'm scared.

Aurore is uncharacteristically stern. —Phélice. And I am talking only to Phélice now. Do not be scared, chouette. You cannot be scared. Look, we are all here to help you. Do not listen to anyone but us. Phélice?

Phélice gives a small nod of assent. Aurore beams back at her, heartened.

—Now Phélice, she continues, —you have been asking about your father and I'm afraid we haven't been very helpful up to now, have we? Clémence told us all about your dreams this last while, and the trouble with Pierre. Well, everything is tied up and explained in those dreams. The dreams where you see people, ah, raped and, and killed. Your father is there, in those pictures.

—Shut your hole, labours Phélice, each word an effort. She drags heavily on her cigarette.

Léonie tries to hide her fear by lowering her voice. —I don't like this, she says hesitantly. —Go away, she adds quickly.

—Go away, mimics Phélice, closing her eyes.

Why are you still so angry and so hateful? wonders Léonie.

Phélice rocks her chair back and turns her head from Clémence's voice.

—Je Vous salut Marie, pleine de grâce. Le Seigneur est avec Vous. Vous êtes bénite entre toute les femmes et Jésus le fruit de vos entrailles est bénit. Sainte Marie, Mère de Dieu, priez pour nous pécheurs . . .

Clémence's words are clear. Léonie's face becomes set and grim.

–Phélice, this is important, says Léonie, the fear purged from her words.
–This has gone on much too long—the Morin, the Massie, and the Trefflé,
side by side for hundreds of years, fighting and hiding and coming out to
fight again. Some is gone with the older ones, with Philia and Baptiste.
Some is gone with Pierre and your no-babies, all our no-babies, she says,
looking tenderly at Diane, Aurore, and Clémence.

–No babiessss, hisses Phélice, rocking forward, her eyes flashing.

–We are too old for this foolishness, sighs Aurore. –Why did Philia ever put
up with this? I'll never know . . .

Marie twists her napkin under the table. –She couldn't ask Patrique or Léo
to help, they didn't do this. Then Delphis died and, well . . . she trails off.

–Well, she could have asked us, sniffs Diane, –we don't live so far that we
couldn't have made the trip!

Phélice's eyes glisten and she licks her lips. –Tell me a story, she wheezes,
scratching herself lazily on the insides of her wrists, cigarette dangling from
her lips.

Clémence prays quietly in the background, –Amen. Je Vous salut Marie
pleine de grâce . . .

Léonie reaches for Philia's scrapbook. She opens it to the inside of the front
cover.

This time I will tell her everything, thinks Léonie. I no longer have to
choose my words carefully. I no longer have to hide.

She speaks calmly, having rehearsed the words she is about to speak every
year since Phélice first asked about her father.

–We are the Morin from Riviere-du-Renard Gaspé, le talon, the heel of
Québec. Your arrière grand-père Marc was the husband of Rubis Caillou,
your grand-père Raoul's mother. Raoul was the father of Mémère Philia
Massie. The Caillou, the Morin, and the Massie go back a long way together.
Remember that, she says, firmly drawing her finger over the lines of the
family tree drawn there in dark-blue, almost-black ink.

Our family left the Gaspé after the trouble with Rubis and the Trefflés. We can't know for sure, but Baptiste Trefflé let it slip, more than once, that it was Trefflés who killed Rubis . . . something about a stillborn birth. They blamed her for it, condemned her, and denounced her as a witch, drowned her.

Léonie sighs, —You'd think, well, you'd think that would make him ashamed, knowing his family did that but . . .

Madelaine snaps, —Ashamed? Him? Baptiste was evil. He was crazy! What about Louise? What about that, einh? And Clémence there, he tried to set the fire on her! So crazy! Hated his own children with a passion. The killing was in him, as it was in his family before him . . . she mutters on, reaching for the cigarettes and lighting it expertly. She sits there, puffing and glaring at Phélice.

Léonie shakes her head, —Yes, the killing was in him. Brutal man, made brutal children . . . Reuville was hard too. He took me, hard and brutal like that, with fists and hisses, me nothing more than a lump, all crying and snot and no voice. I walked around for the longest time feeling like someone had smacked me on the back of the head with a frying pan. I was fifteen years old. What did I know?

—I knew nothing about Rubis or how Baptiste was involved, I was fifteen and so damned ugly, well, I thought Reuville loved me, she says simply. —I thought, to do that, he must love me.

—He was so beautiful. I thought that maybe, maybe with enough time and love, I could get him to love me, even just a little bit. I thought maybe I could erase some of that hate from his eyes, some of the scars from his body . . .

She looks up at Diane, who nods sympathetically.

—We had to get married. I wouldn't let Maman Philia take that away from me. It was a chance to prove that someone could love me. But, she says, —that baby died inside me. In death it became even more like Reuville, like Baptiste. It was angry and wanted to hurt me. Marie could not stop the bleeding for a couple of weeks. We buried that poor hump of blood and bones in the bush, back behind Madelaine and Aurore's place. A beautiful place all full of flowers . . .

—Lilies of the valley, says Clémence in mid-prayer.

—Yes, that's right, Léonie says, a fleeting smile on her lips, smelling the flowers once more. Taking a deep breath, she continues. —The next two babies were too close together. You, Phélice, were barely a year old when your brother was born.

Phélice becomes agitated. Her voice greedy, angry, —Boy! Yes, my boy!

Léonie stares angrily at her.

—It was about then that I started losing my hair. People thought it was from having the babies so close together. You were still young and Joseph was the type to cry most all the time. They had said that I couldn't get pregnant while I still nursed you, but my milk made you sick. You didn't nurse long. I didn't have enough milk for Joseph either.

—But you know, that hair didn't just fall out by itself, Phélice, she leans menacingly towards her daughter.

She puts her hands flat on the table and rises slightly from her chair, —It was from Reuville, yanking it whenever he walked by, by the handfuls, to get my attention. He said having babies around made me too slow and stupid to hear him the first time. But I was quick enough to get you kids from the bed when I heard him coming though, einh? I wasn't stupid *or* deaf, just tired of listening to him, that's all!

She stands facing Phélice, her voice sharp, —Lucky for me, he stayed at his dad's place most the day, coming home long enough to bother me, then pass out in his own piss and vomit. It wasn't like I could go back home, she laughs harshly. "You made your bed, lie in it," was all Philia would say to me.

—I did all the work around the place and depended a lot on the goodness of others. It was hard, you know, to take charity like that, but it was that or lose you kids. I did what I had to do. She finishes and sits back heavily on her chair.

—Now Léonie, you know we did all we could to help, soothes Diane. —Paul and I were more than happy to help out at the store, and Joe and Robert were always up at your place, fixing the roof or setting fence rails . . .

–I know, I know, sighs Léonie irritably, pinching the bridge of her nose and squeezing her eyes shut. –And I know it was hard to get around Philia too, I know that. She had such a hatred for the Trefflés . . .

–And with good reason, says Madelaine, butting out her cigarette and crossing her arms over her chest. She gives Reuville her best cue-de-poule.

Léonie holds up her hand to stop the others from talking. –Philia had such a hatred of the Trefflés that when I was pregnant again she asked if I wanted to be, you know, not pregnant.

Clémence's head jerks up from her rosary.

Léonie pretends not to notice and continues, –She was ready to help me, to forgive me, she said, because she knew I couldn't survive another baby. It was, Léonie sighs, –a tough decision to make. My mother was asking me to choose between my husband and her.

–But, she grimaces, –I had already made my choice by marrying him. Maman already knew that too, I suppose.

–I was four months pregnant when I started to bleed. I knew I was losing the baby and in a way, it sounds awful to say, but I was happy about that. I didn't go to anyone for help. I just kept right on working, hauling the wood, and doing the wash, to help bring it on. I thought, "I'll lose this one and still have Phélice and Joseph, that should keep Reuville happy. Maybe that will make Reuville happy."

–Happy? croaks Phélice, her cigarette dead between her fingers.

–Nothing would have made him happy, Aurore says, shaking her head sadly. –Nothing.

Léonie nods in agreement. –You're right, of course. But I thought that, that maybe, he would see that I was trying. Trying to make him happy! To do what I thought he wanted me to do, to make his shitty father stop hating us, stop hating him . . .

—Nothing would have changed Reuville and the way he beat on you, and nothing would have changed Baptiste, says Diane gently. —He hated Philia so he hated you. Like he hated all of us.

—Hate, says Phélice, looking intently at Léonie, as if seeing her for the first time. —hurts, she snarls.

Léonie reaches for Phélice's hand but Phélice winces and draws back deep within her chair.

Léonie leaves her hand on the table in front of Phélice. She speaks like a strong, clean wind —When the pains got real bad and I was bleeding pretty heavy I remember thinking I was going to die, so I had to bring you and Joseph somewhere safe. I needed to be somewhere safe too, either to die or to be taken care of. I thought of Madelaine. Clémence had snuck over to see me that night after supper, thank God! She knew what was going on . . .

Aurore catches Diane's eye.

— So I sent her to tell Madelaine that I was coming.

Au clair de la lune,
Pierrot repondit:
Je n'ai pas de plume,
Je suis dans mon lit.
Va chez la voisine:
Je crois qu'elle y est,
Car dans sa cuisine
On bat le briquet.

There is hardly any light outside, only a crescent moon, sharp in the night sky. The wind worries the shingles on the roof, like stubborn scabs over a half-healed wound.

Inside the house it is dark and the stove is cold. Reuville staggers into the kitchen and drops a heavy bag onto the floor. Léonie shuffles in from the side bedroom. She is bent nearly double, fumbling and clutching at a great wad of bedclothes stained with blood. In obvious pain, she lowers herself into a chair and lays her head on the table. With one hand she beckons Reuville.

Reuville reaches for the bottle in front of her. He drinks deeply then knocks the bottle three times against her skull. Her arm curls protectively around her head, then her hand goes out again, towards him, to protest, to keep him away, to draw him closer.

He yanks her head back by the roots of her hair and forces the bottle between her lips.

Léonie cries out. Arms flailing wildly, she throws herself onto the floor.

Reuville nudges the bag with his foot, drawing it closer to Léonie's prone body. He picks it up, swings it in front of her, and threatens to let it fall on top of her.

Léonie scrabbles to her feet. Crying out, she turns round to go back to the bedroom, then back towards the door to outside. At every turn Reuville strikes her body with the bag. He slaps her face with one hand, goads her with whatever mewls from the sack with the other.

Léonie finally stumbles against the stove. Bracing herself against the cold metal, her hand touches the poker. She clutches the weight of it and whirls, smacking the sack with a strength and a fury that are not hers.

Reuville dangles the sack for a minute, watching with fascination the stain that is spreading through the cloth. Suddenly, as if it burns him, he lets it drop. The sack lands heavily between them. A small white hand spills from the neck of the bag.

Léonie, chest heaving, stares transfixed by the weight of that tiny hand. She seems to want to bend down towards it. In the same instant, she lifts the poker again and with a strangled cry, swings it towards Reuville's head. He falls against the table and slumps to the floor.

—He told me that he had found the biggest goddamned rat's nest out at his dad's earlier that day. He said it was in the sack for me. I didn't know it was Joseph in that sac, whispers Léonie. —How could I know? she her anguished face to her family. —When he was on the ground, I left, made it as far as Diane's.

Léonie blows her nose. —I killed your brother, Phélice, and I killed your dad for making me do that. I killed him that night. And he will hate me forever, he will never love me, Léonie finishes fiercely.

Madelaine raps the empty teacup on the table in front of her. —Léonie, she says firmly, you didn't kill Reuville. That little knock on the head wouldn't have killed a dog. Diane called us over that night. None of us were asleep. Aurore had told us that you were going to need help. We went and got Philia and Delphis. Then we went to get Reuville.

circle of light moving kerosene smell
see black boots, heels worn at the back, brown shoes, scruffy shoes
standing close feet smell

—Well, quite the mess isn't he?

—Is he dead?

Aurore crouches beside Reuville, tentatively puts two fingers to the side of his neck.

—No, she sighs, not dead . . .

—Out cold though. Léonie got that part right, at least.

—And this, whispers Aurore, carefully lifting and cradling the sack bearing Joseph.

—What do you think? rasps Delphis, nudging Reuville with the toe end of his boot.

Philia rights the knocked over chair. —We should clean up, she says quietly.

—Yes, agrees Marie, pushing up her sleeves, —Bloodstains are so bad. We need to get to this before it dries.

—Not the blood, snaps Philia, —This! She prods the groaning Reuville with distaste. —He's starting to come around. We need him out of this house.

—Well now, I don't know that Evelyn would like to see this tonight, drawls Delphis, setting his rifle on the table.

—We're not taking him there, Philia says impatiently. —We are cleaning up this mess.

Delphis looks at his wife and shakes his head. Madelaine stands beside Aurore.

—Listen to me, all of you, even you, pig! Philia commands, prodding Reuville again with her shoe. —Léonie has suffered for this mistake of a marriage, this sin. Joseph and Phélice, well, Phélice, she says more quietly, —Phélice and Léonie will never face this again. Not while I'm alive. Delphis, get him up. Keep the gun on him. Aurore, yes, you can keep the baby for now, but you will have to come with us. We need everyone for this.

She walks over to the door. —Come on.

Marie looks suspiciously at Philia. —What do you mean? What are you saying? Tell me, say it.

Philia narrows her eyes but does not speak.

Marie's hand covers her mouth. —No, she whispers. Then louder, —No, Philia, no! Hasn't there been enough blood spilled? Enough blood for three lifetimes! We can't just . . .

—We're not going to spill any blood, idiot. We are going to stop it.

Aurore moans and clutches the bloodied sack even tighter, burrowing her face into the cloth.

Madelaine's eyes open wide. She puts out her hand to protest, and then slowly steps over Reuville to stand beside Philia.

—She's right, says Madelaine softly. —We know she's right. This won't shed blood. She continues eagerly, —Marie, you could drown him. I can break him. We all can do something for Léonie, for Phélice, she falters, then blurts out, —Rubis drowned. Rubis was drowned. This has to be. Yes, it has to be this way.

—But, pleads Marie, —if we do this, we're no better than him, she looks pityingly at Reuville, now swaying upright, leaning against Delphis's right arm. — No better than Baptiste or them that killed Mémère Rubis! Don't you see this?

—No better, no worse, snaps Philia. There was no judge there when Rubis died. No law.

—But we will lose it all! It is wrong to turn against the gifts . . .

—Who are you to say that? Philia says, her voice low, a tight, controlled fury building inside her. —Who are you to judge right and wrong, Marie? Will you judge Léonie for what happened here tonight? Einh? Will you judge me? Answer me that. Remember why you have the gift, ma fille. You have it to make things right. Now come on, all of you.

Aurore and Marie stand together. Madelaine turns the handle and pushes the door open. A cool breeze blows in. Delphis and Philia shoulder the burden of Léonie's drunk husband between them. They exchange a look. Delphis shifts Reuville a bit, leans over, and picks up the rifle. They shoulder their way through the door and out into the night. Marie sighing, picks up the lantern and puts her arm around Aurore. Together they step through the door. Marie pauses to shut the door, leaving the house to its darkness.

together, then two behind
grim face Delphis on one side
rifle bumping my thigh

Philia eyes of ice
poking and pushing

Can' walk no fashter woman. Jéshush, where you takin' me? Party maybe?
Little party, einh?

They stop when they reach the stand of trees and willow bush that separates
the back of the yard from the field that belongs to the Trefflés. Through the
trees, they can see the yard light Evelyn had installed after Baptiste died.
—To keep others from getting lost, mutters Philia, crossing herself. She feels
Reuville's body stiffen as he recognizes the spot.

Delphis is quick to untangle himself when the younger man begins to
vomit. He keeps his eyes averted but the gun is steady as he lowers Reuville
to the ground. Reuville stays there crouching on all fours, coughing and
spitting.

what? here? this is the bush. if Maman sees . . . oh shit! empty it out, that's
it, get it out. you'll feel better, that's it. maybe just sleep it off here then,
einh? is that it? you bring me here to sleep, einh? scritchy scratchy this, but
okay. ouch! whoa there! don't talk so fuckin' loud einh? who? Rubis? what
the . . . killed her? don' even fuckin' know no Rubis. no, no! not Joseph, not
me for sure, that one. it was Léonie, her, she did that. don't know know
what? where is she? make her stay here, all scratchy hey. stop saying that.
what the hell is this? I'm getting out of here, I . . . ah, oh.

barrel of a rifle

all shoes scrunching crunching now quiet, so quiet. gone?

I'll move my finger a little to

oh, ah okay.

shoes quiet, boots quiet now
still so
quiet
oh?
whaaat th- . . . ah . . .

Delphis keeps the gun on him but he doesn't need to really.
We stop the blood then we make the fire come.

> The fire rages and boils bones.
> We hear the final crack of bones, skin giving up.
> We bring the water up in him.

> We leave that Dark One in the bush,
> not enough man in him left to bury.
> Leave him for the magpies,
> the coyote bitches.
> and their babies.

—All that power from God, continues Marie, looking straight into Phélice's eyes, —we poured into that sick animal, cowering, drunk, pissing and shitting himself there in the bush.

Madelaine takes Phélice's hands roughly in her own, looks deep into her eyes. —It was our responsibility. To protect our family.

Phélice pulls her hands away. —Femmes, she scowls, her eyes hooded.

Léonie looks with disbelief at the women.

—Evelyn figured her boy ran away that night, like Roland had run away. I thought Dad and you had buried Reuville. You never told me he wasn't dead. You never told me I didn't kill him. Why didn't you tell me I didn't kill him? Why didn't you tell me I wasn't responsible? She slams her fist down on top of Philia's book.

Diane says quietly, —You were responsible. And you needed to believe that you paid the debt on Joseph's death.

She turns to Phélice, —Phélice, I don't know if "I'm sorry" is the thing to say. All I can tell you is that our responsibility was to protect our family. That's enough for me. That should be enough for you, she finishes, decisively slapping shut Philia's book, Rubis's book, and every photo album on the table.

She pushes the pile of books into the centre of the table, pauses, then pushes it towards Phélice.

Phélice's eyes lock on the books. She pales. —Famille? she mutters anxiously. Looking around at the women, Phélice cocks her head questioningly. She can hear another voice. —Rubis? she whispers hoarsely.

She starts to shake, like someone who has been out in the cold too long.

—Famille, she mumbles. She draws a deep, shuddering breath. Her head falls to her chest. The glow leaks from her eyes, tears milky-smoke from a dying fire.

Léonie whispers, —They can fix anyone, she reaches for Phélice's hand, —even your dad.

She gets up and stands beside Phélice, cups her daughter's chin, and kisses her tenderly on the forehead.

Madelaine pours a last drink from the bottle into the teacup and drains it.

—I think she needs to sleep now, says Aurore, getting up. —I will make up the spare bed.

—I'll help you, says Clémence, kissing the rosary and handing it back to Madelaine.

Léonie bends to hug her daughter about the waist. Madelaine helps her stand.

There is a banging on the porch, the door opens, and the men come in slowly, sniffing the air apprehensively.

—So? You girls been drinking, einh? smiles Paul, looking over at Phélice being half-carried by Léonie and Madelaine down the hallway.

—Drinking and telling dirty stories, I suppose?

—Something like that, smiles Diane, looking up. She holds out her hand to her husband.

les mèches de cheveux

you're in the bath
and you remember the scar it was there
but you can't see it anymore
and wonder
left leg?

right leg?

and you open the door—
it moans in the hallway of memories

you play back the night he
took a stick from the fire
and you think
left leg?

Aurore and Madelaine in the dark bedroom at Philia's:

–It's all right, you can talk now.

–

–Is there anything you want to say? Anything?

–

–Rubis?

–

–Well, that's all right then. You don't have to say anything.

–

–She's gone then?

–I can't hear her.

–Bonsoir Aurore.

–Bonsoir Madelaine.

Marie and Diane whispering in the dark hallway between bedrooms at Marie's house:

–Bonsoir Marie.

–Bonsoir Diane. Diane? Did you know Reuville would do that? Come back, I mean?

–Non, I didn't know.

–That was rude.

–Yes, but then he was always was crass.

–Yes, such poor taste really. I'm glad Dad wasn't here to see that.

–Yes.

–Diane?

–Yes?

–Will he come back again?

–No, I don't think so Marie. I think this time he is gone.

–Do you really?

–

–Diane?

–I don't know, Marie. I pray he is.

–I'll pray too.

–That's good. Bonsoir enfant de Dieu.

–Bonsoir mon ange.

Clémence and Robert in the dark:

–Then what happened?

–Then he left and you men came back in.

–Whew! No wonder Phélice was so wiped out. I thought she was drunk,
you know?

–I know.

–I guess . . .

–You guess what?

–I guess, I mean, I don't suppose you'll tell anyone about, about Léonie
and, well, the others? What they did to Reuville, I mean?

–Who would I tell, Robert? Who would you tell?

–I was just thinking your mom might like to know, maybe, what happened
to her son and all.

–Philia was my mother.

–No, I mean Evelyn.

–No, I won't tell her.

–Do you think anyone else will?

–No, I don't think so. It wouldn't make any difference now, would it?

—What about the rest of them? The other Trefflés? Should they know?

—Robert, I'm sure they have their own version of the past.

—So it's not for us to tell them?

—Non, that's for someone else.

—Okay, Clémence, okay. You're the boss.

—Go to sleep, mon vieux, morning comes early and we have to drive Aurore and Madelaine to the airport.

—I thought Patrique was driving them?

—No, Léonie needs him to straighten out some floorboards at Mom's.

—Okay lady, whatever you say. Bonsoir Clémence. I love you.

—I love you too, Robert, bonsoir bonhomme.

A small dust-coloured spider weaves a web from corner to wall above their heads. For her, the work is endless.

Edmonton 1963

Through the long night-watches,
May thine angels spread
Their white wings above me
Watching round my bed.

Bonsoir Raoul

x Maman

Phélice smiles and closes Rubis's book. She takes a pen from the coffee cup. First she doodles what looks like a tornado, to get the ink going. Then, in dark-blue, almost black-ink, she writes on the front cover of her own book: *In the end, what we need to survive is maimed, burnt, and broken but refuses to be forgotten.*

🖼 Translations

The following terms are, for the most part, colloquial expressions.

A ta santé – To your health

Ah bien – Ah well

bapteme – baptism

bas de laine – knitted wool socks

belle-mère – mother-in-law

bec pincé – see *cu-de-poule*

bonhomme – (my) good man

chérie – cherished one

chouette – baby owl; term of endearment

cu-de-poule – literally, a chicken's anus; refers to someone's mouth being
pinched in disapproval

curé – a priest

diable – the devil, Satan

dons – various abilities to heal or to reduce pain. Facilitating prayers
were usually passed on from male to female, female to male;
sometimes designated to the seventh child regardless of sex

enfant – child

famille – family

femme – woman

Fête des Rois – celebration after Christmas day to honour the three kings
who journeyed to Bethlehem for Christ's birth

gamin – derivative term for children

Je t'aime – I love you

Je t'embrasse – I am hugging you

Je Vous salut Marie – Hail Mary (Catholic prayer)

l'Abbé – familiar term for a Catholic priest

l'eau de Pâques – water gathered from a running source of natural water
before sunrise on Easter morning; said to have healing properties

ma fille – my girl

ma foie du bon Dieu – my faith in God; my goodness

ma tante – my aunt

maître chez-nous – master in our own house

maître de sa misère – to become master over one's affliction

maman – mother

mémère – grandmother

mon oncle – my uncle

mon vieux – my old man

ôtes-toi du chemin – get out of the way

pied bot – club foot

piquée – homemade cloth diaper

pour faire une tresse, assemblez trois longues mèches de cheveux – to make a braid, separate the hair into three equal strands

Qu'le diable les prends – The devil take them

quand même – all the same

ragotte – whiskey made by filling empty whiskey barrels with water. After a time, the whiskey leeches out of the barrel's wood into the water.

rameau – palm leaves blessed on Palm Sunday; said to have protective properties

réveillon – celebration after Christmas midnight mass that lasts until sunrise

sauvage – literally, a savage or someone wild

tabernacle – an ornamental locked box fixed to the middle of the altar and used for holding the host

une pour la raison – one for reason

une pour l'action – one for action

une pour l'âme – one for the soul

vas-y fille – go-ahead girl

vièrge – virgin

J'entends le moulin (**I Hear the Mill Wheel**) – **Traditional**

> Father is building us a house,
> I hear the mill wheel, tack-a,
> There are three gables on our house, tick-a tack-a, tick-a tack-a.
>
> I hear the mill wheel, tick-a tick-a tack-a,
> I hear the mill wheel, tack-a.

Un Canadien errant – Traditional

Once a Canadian lad,
Exiled from hearth and home,

Wandered alone and sad,
Through alien lands unknown.

Down by a rushing stream,
Thoughtful and sad one day,
He watched the water pass and to it he did say:
"If you should reach my land,
My most unhappy land,
Please speak to all my friends
So they will understand.
Tell them how much I wish
That I could be once more
In my beloved land
That I will see no more.

Tell them I remember."

C'est le matin – Paulette Dubé

It is the morning
and the sun is rising
glistening on the back of the day moon.

All the birds
are still in their cradles.
Water and wind are speaking—

It is the whisper of God
It is the smile of God
It is the promise of God.

Au clair de la lune – Traditional

By the clear moonlight,
My friend Pierrot,
Lend me your quill to write a few words.
My candle is dead, my fireplace cold,
Open your door to me,
For the love of God.

By the clear moonlight,
Pierrot replies:
I have no quill,
I am in bed.
Go to the neighbour's:
I believe she is still awake,
Because I see firelight through her kitchen window.
In his feather bed,
Pierrot falls asleep.
He dreams of the Moon:
His heart beats fulfilled
Because of Her infinite love
For the child dressed in white,
The moon gives him a croissant of silver.

Auprès de ma blonde – Traditional

Refrain:

Next to my girlfriend
How good it is
Next to my girlfriend
How good it is to sleep.

Mon tour va venir un jour – Adam Hebert

(ARRANGEMENT: BARACHOIS, RAÔUL DUGUAY & GREY LARSEN/PUBLISHED BY FLAT TOWN MUSIC)

My turn will come some day
It doesn't matter what you say
You can leave me and go your way
But my turn will come one day

Every night chasing what you want
You must know you're doing wrong
You're leaving me to run around
But my turn will come some day
You have another by your side
And I'm afraid what's done is done
You left me to run around
But my turn will come some day

Le Forgeron, Bonhomme! Bonhomme! – Traditional

See how the blacksmith shapes the steel,
He shapes the steel,
He shapes the steel.

Mon mari est bien malade – Traditional

My husband is gravely ill
In great danger of dying.
He sent me to fetch some wine
The best to be found in Paris.

I love you so, now and then,
I love you so, my man.

He sent me to fetch some wine
The best to be found in Paris.
When I reached the mountains high
I heard the bell toll for him.

When I reached the mountains high

I heard the bell toll for him.
I grabbed my basket full of silver coins
Quickly, I ran back.

Upon arriving home
I found my husband dead,
shrouded, laid out.
I grabbed him by the leg
To my garden I dragged him.

I grabbed him by the leg
To my garden I dragged him.
I called the pigeons and the crows:
Come and eat, it's my husband!

En roulant ma boule – **Traditional**

Playing with my ball, rolling it along.
Behind our house we have a pond.
There I roll my ball,
Where three fine ducks swim 'round and 'round.

Where three fine ducks swim 'round and 'round
To hunt them comes the young king's son.

To hunt them comes the young king's son.
With him he brings his shining gun.

With him he brings his shining gun.
He aims at the black for fun,
But then he hits the whitest one.

He aims at the black for fun,
But then he hits the whitest one.
Oh, prince, you are wicked!

Une petite chandelle – Paulette Dubé

A little candle, I light tonight.
A little candle to chase the night.
A little candle to make things right.
A little candle I light tonight.
Flame the colour of honey, my lovely little candle.
Lights up all the sky, my sweet lovely little candle.

Notre maman du ciel – Traditional

We have, in heaven
a sainted mother.
It is the Mother of God,
It is the Virgin Marie.

Oh gentle Mother,
to you we give our love.
On this earth
be our saving grace.

Protect your children,
keep us innocent.
Guide our trembling steps
and be our guiding light.

Acknowledgements

Gros becs to:

Alice Dubé, Lucille Dubé, Simonne Blanchette, Marcel Dubé, and Bella Beaupré, for sharing their memories;

to Don McKay, who taught me the difference between a good mystery and a bad mystery;

to John Weier, for showing me the difference between "is waking" and "wakes";

to Louise SkyDancer Halfe, for teaching me that most dreams are sent with good intent, and for her silver sharp eyes;

to Thomas Wharton who taught me how to write a novel;

and especially to the Titan Twelve, who never let go and who never forgot.

This book is for Raymond, who taught me what it means to trust and for André, whose presence is the very meaning of healing.

Les bénédictions de ma famille, Paulette Dubé.

PAULETTE DUBÉ was born in Westlock, Alberta, and grew up in the French village of Legal. When she was three, she watched her third sister being born on the kitchen table and has been hooked on magic, creation, and miracles ever since.

Paulette is the author of three books and the recipient of a number of awards, including the Milton Acorn Memorial People's Poetry Award (1994) and the CBC Alberta Anthology (1998). Selections from *Talon* were shortlisted for the 1999 Canadian Literary Awards. She is currently a resident of Jasper, Alberta, where she lives with her husband Raymond and her son André.